STORIES

I TOLD

MY DEAD

LOVER

STORIES
I TOLD
MY DEAD
LOVER

Jo Paquette

BLACK
STONE
PUBLISHING

This one's for me

Desire is about vanishing. You dream a
bowl of cherries and next day receive a
letter written in red juice.

—Anne Carson,
Norma Jeane Baker of Troy

Give a monster a name, tell me it prays,
does that make it any less a monster?

—Joshua McCune, *Invisible Monsters*

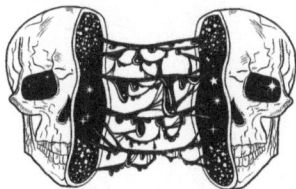

We're not combatants, call the violinists;
we're not victims, either, add the violas.
We're just humans, sing the cellos, *just
humans: flawed and beautiful and aching
for love.*

—Susan Cain, *Bittersweet*

CONTENTS

LEFT TURN
AT THE LOST SOUL

They said later it was the kind of place you had to be lost in order to find, said it like there was some mystical force at work driving things, driving us, moving people around like chess pieces on a board. Something like fate.

Fate? Don't make me laugh.

You can call it fate or luck or anything in between. Me, I am for none of those things. I'm for life, for grit, for putting one foot after another on the tightrope of life, and just hoping you don't clip your own wings back too far before the plunge.

———

It was a dry-heave August, had been since day one, the world a tinderbox set to explode. I had to get away. I just had to get away: from my summer writing prof and his constant pressure to apply myself, from the auto repair shop as herald of my limitless potential, even from Alyssa, who honestly tried but who were we kidding really? And so one night, with the butt end of the month egging me on and a dozen calls I could not find it in me to return, I got into my car and just drove. No goal, no destination, no map. I made the road my fuse and I flung myself like a lit match and I blew.

I ran out of gas somewhere in South Dakota. My '98 Mustang sputtered and coughed a bit, gave a good effort, but I knew it for what it was. If I'd put on my brain with my ball cap before heading out, I would have filled that spare gas canister rattling around the trunk, or at least kept an eye on the gauge. But no dice. Now I was bone dry and only moonlight on tumbleweeds to tell the tale.

What could I do? I hefted the canister under my arm and I walked.

I make a point of not marking the time, or at least back then I did. What good's it do to know when it is, when it was, when it will be? Things that need doing will make themselves known in their own time, that's what my pop used to say, and I've never seen any reason to think different.

So I couldn't say how long I went at it. But eventually I hit a patch of houses, every one of them spit-gray under the uneasy moon, no sooner seen than forgotten. I put the big sky and its ring of gathering storm clouds behind me and I hugged that tumbleweed road and I walked on.

It was the shadow that rose up first, rose black in my side vision like some altar to insanity. You let your mind out alone in the dimmet and just see what bones it throws back at your feet. Mine? It brought me this god-awful dead husk that must once have been a tree: thick-bodied trunk flanked by two tall, supplicating limbs, spearing up at the night like nothing so much as a lost soul. The road split off in two directions, and is it really a choice when you are not aware of making it?

For no reason but whim I went left.

———

WELCOME TO KISMET, the sign said. POPULATION . . . I couldn't tell you. I couldn't tell you because that part of the sign was torn clean off, gashed right through the corrugated metal. By now, the light was dwindling. Massing clouds ate the moon, bite upon bite. The prestorm air was combustible, crackling, full of violence to come.

You could go all signs and symbols here, tangle the strings of fate with my shoelaces to explain why I kept on walking: past the houses, past the general store, past the gas station, right to the edge of what passed for town. But is it fate when the hard edge of night means everything else is shut, so you just keep on toward that one lit sign naysaying the dark?

Fate or dumb luck, you tell me. All I know is, I saw it and I came on.

The joint rose out of the dust, an unlikely oasis. Creaky roof and blow-me-down walls, a strip of asphalt out back with a couple rattletrap wheelers, and over it all an enormous pink-and-lavender sign: KISMET CAFÉ & VACANCIES. Just below in smaller, blinking cursive: Don't Be a Stranger.

The room I entered was all smoke and dust and the future ghosts of memories not yet made. There was a grungy bar on the right with three or four empty stools in front. The farthest one turned very slowly in place. On the left, a couple of tables, each with a rickety chair or two. Somewhere an ancient jukebox played "Hotel California," and I didn't think I had ever been home before this moment, though I couldn't have told you why. The front door swung shut on distant thunder and the rest of the world disappeared.

My feet found their way to the nearest stool. A grizzled barman slammed me down a glass of amber and I was young enough not to know and old enough not to care. I threw it back and scanned the room. Then the back door opened and there she was, one slim exclamation mark answering a question I hadn't even known to ask.

She leaned over the jukebox. She trailed a finger down the top, paused, pushed, pulled back in satisfaction. A new melody curled out like smoke. I stood. She turned: short hair scuffed around her face, arms carving up the shadows, bare feet and ankles under the rolled-up cuffs of low-slung jeans. I saw her see me. Whatever had brought me here was a relic from another life, gone and forgotten. Just empty hands now clenching, unclenching.

I took one step toward her. I stopped. She raised her chin and one round flat earring caught the neon window light and splashed it across her face like a premonition. The room was empty or maybe it wasn't, maybe the world was barren but for just us two, maybe I never believed in fate until this moment. Maybe I should have known better.

Now she would keep coming toward me. She had that look in her eye and this was her space and who was

I to go reading symbols? But she didn't. She stood and she stayed and she swayed in the swelling music, jukebox as orchestra of the gods or was that just the sound of my next Jack hitting the counter? One arm swung to her opposite hip and the other to the other as she closed her eyes and let the beat tug her, one thrum, one curl, one muscle at a time. A thin red cord looped her neck and hung down between her breasts as she swayed side to side to side.

She didn't come any closer. I didn't either. Yet moments later there we were. She was so near I could taste her, sweat and soap and sex tangled in her night hair, rolling off her skin in waves. I let it come. I let it all come. I kept my hands at my sides and shuffled one foot, then the other. I'd never wanted to be a dancer before this moment.

She leaned in. She rested one wrist flat on my collarbone, the lightest electric jolt. She flung her head back and around and around, baring her long neck as it flashed pink and blue and mauve in the blinking light filtering in from outside.

I did move, then. I had to or I'd burst. Just one hand to start, so easy on her waist, then the next as she pushed into me, arching against my chest just as sweet as an ache. I pulled her close and she looked up, her eyes all questions and her lips tilted in a hint of devil-may-care. I cupped the back of her neck, felt the knotted cord rough on my palm, leaned in.

Then it was over.

The music stopped and she stopped and we were no longer alone. Hard-drinking guy over here, insomniac housewife over there, grizzled bartender looking inscrutable and if we weren't the talk of the town, we were sure the look of it.

These are the moments anticlimax is made for. I didn't care. I cleared my throat of a silence that had maybe lasted my whole life.

"Hey," I said. Just that: "Hey."

She considered me. She leaned in close to my ear, and that voice—I can hear it still; that voice, as rough as whiskey and it burned all the way down; that voice—she said, "You need to go."

She turned and she pushed through the far door and disappeared.

The barman slammed a glass on the counter behind me. I grabbed it blind and gulped it down without a thought.

Go? I was already gone.

———

Next thing I knew I was swapping stories at the bar with a wizened Methuselah who'd boosted his stool with an honest-to-god phone book for a better fit. I was flying too high to much care but not too high to appreciate the finer strands of human ingenuity. Bill, his name was, but he went by Old Sassafras and who was I to say different? He asked me how I came to Kismet and he perked right up when I described the old burned-out lost soul of a tree I'd passed in my coming.

"Ah, yeah. Quite a sight, that one is. Came out all this way, did ya? That's a long walk for such a little pecker."

There didn't seem to be a right answer to what wasn't even a question, so I settled for the truth. "I needed gas."

Old Sassafras grunted. "Gone and left off your can now, did ya?"

I waved vaguely back toward the street outside. I mean, it had to be out there somewhere. I'd had it till I hadn't, and wasn't that just the way of things?

My companion was back to musing. "Lost soul, eh? I like that," he said. "You know, it used to be a fine tree, years ago. A fine tall tree. Got hit by lightning, so it did. I saw it with my own eyes: one big arc from the sky and boom. There you go. Lost soul!" He chuckled and burped.

I downed the rest of my swill.

"So," he said.

"So?"

He looked meaningfully at the far door. *Her* door.

It hadn't occurred to me before that moment that I could just follow her, that UNAUTHORIZED PERSONS KEEP OUT did not necessarily mean me. But I was young then, I was young and I was dumb and I did not yet understand the nature of obsession, how it is a jealous bird that mates for life and does not leave its prey alive. I was still in the neon blindness stage. I would learn.

But in that moment, I went stone-cold sober. Was it too late? Could I just?

I turned back to Old Sass, but he was deep in his cup. The bartender was busy at the sink. Everybody in the room had somewhere they had to be.

And so did I.

————

The back door didn't open onto a storeroom or parking garage or the empty lot I'd have imagined, if I'd taken the time to imagine anything at all. No. It was a garden, right out of a damn storybook, all ivy-covered stone walls and perfumed flowers and everywhere *green*—a green I could see even through the darkness. What was this place?

A flagstone path cut through the careful grass and I followed it, my labored breath the only sound. The moon was gone now, the black sky a great gunpowder bowl ready to blow. I would have called for her, but I didn't even know her name.

Another minute and I found her on a decorative bench, perched up on its back with one foot on the seat and the other on the armrest. A prick of light glinted off something she held—a blade?—as she worked a creamy lump that was cupped in her other hand.

Her gaze flicked up as I got nearer. One side of her mouth curved in a smile. She might have said, *Took you long enough.* Instead she said, "You ever play that game as a kid, 'Would you rather'?"

"Sure. Would you rather feel a stab every time you blink your eyes or be forced to take in all your food through a hole in your stomach?"

She laughed low. "First one. Obviously. Would you rather have oozing sores all over your body or walk everywhere on your hands for a year?"

"Last one for sure. I mean, hello, infection?" Then, "What you got going there?"

She hopped off the bench. She wiped the knife on

her jeans, snapped it shut, slid it into a pocket. Then she tossed the lump at me, underhand, and I surprised myself by catching it. A bell? It was intricately carved with loops and curlicues, the surface instantly going oozy and slick in my sweaty grip.

I looked up, surprised. "Soap?"

She was already walking away. She called over her shoulder: "Come on."

Out in this dome of night, her voice was less fire and more smoke. I let it fill my lungs.

A small clearing abutted the garden wall. "Over here," she said. "Look," she said. And I saw. There were dozens of soap carvings scattered all along and on and in the stone wall: a tiny bridge, a spiky high-heeled shoe, a disembodied ear, a small carved saucer topped with a scatter of tiny intricately rendered pills. I set the bell in the spot where she directed me. Then I stood next to her as she considered—what? Her hobby? Her kingdom? The world's kitschiest outdoor talent show?

She pointed to the stiletto. "Can't wear 'em. Old ligament tear. And this," a paintbrush, "I used to love painting—landscapes, portraits, you name it. Still have no idea why I stopped. A buddy I know lost an ear to a dog. My dog." She stroked a small, intricate pit bull. Then a fringed beach towel topped with a pair of

11

sunglasses. "I always wanted to see the ocean. Stretches to the end of the world, isn't that what they say?"

"I don't get it," I said, because it needed saying. "You carve all this stuff out of soap and then you just leave it outside? What about when it rains?"

She grinned like I was the funniest thing in the world. "It never just rains here. It's bone dry or it pours. Nothing in between. And it hasn't poured in ages."

She had to be kidding. "Haven't you seen the clouds? They've been stoking up the whole day. The sky's ready to burst." Thunder snapped my sentence shut like punctuation.

I waited for her to show concern. But her grin was all teeth. "Why'd you think I called you out here?"

My gaze caught on a flat soap carving that lay on the low stone wall: a puzzle with a dozen interlocking pieces, and one piece missing right in the middle. "As I recall, you told me to go away."

"Did I?" She turned and met me face-on, for one hard second holding nothing back.

And then it came. One drop first, then six, and then—oh, then.

She'd been right. That rain. It wasn't and then it was, it was and it was and it was, like a giant blade gutting the fabric of the sky and tearing out its heart and all that lifeblood raining down, a killing torrent, and all you could do was let it come. Let it come.

She tilted her head back for a long minute, eyes shut to the sky while that trickle turned sheet turned drenching pour. And beside her the wall: no longer stone now but sea, newborn and furious, pocked with exquisite, sudsy crypts.

She never moved to save them. She didn't even try.

I almost intervened. "Do you want me to . . ."

But what could I do, really? What could anyone?

The rain had caught her by surprise, I could tell. But surprise was not what showed on her face. She watched as the storm consumed her memories, her dreams, her regrets. And I watched her. What filled her face, what cascaded down her back and pooled at her feet was not distress, nor was it sorrow, nor loss. It almost looked like . . . joy?

"Don't you mind?" I asked. "All those hours, all that work? It was good, too, all that stuff. You're talented."

She shrugged and pushed her wet hair uselessly back from her forehead. "What can I say? I've always liked the idea of a fresh start."

Then she was moving, then she was on me, tangled in my arms and grabbing at my belt and tearing my sopping shirt up over my head. Her clothes were long gone and I fell back against the moss-rough wall and felt the soap puzzle soften and give against my bare back and I lifted her like she weighed nothing and she wrapped her legs and locked herself in place and how is it that when the torrents come it's always those missing pieces that are the first to fill?

———

In the hot wet dark of after, once the rain had stopped as quick as it began, and we lay tangled in the thick grass now flattened in a ring around us, she spoke into my shoulder. "Did you pass a tree on your way, getting here? An old gutted thing?"

"Two big dead branches reaching up to the sky," I agreed. "Some guy at the bar told me its history."

She was deep in her thoughts. "Everyone likes to tell how it got that way. It's true it didn't used to be this . . . husk. It was a king of a thing once, big and tall and proud. Even I can remember it like that, just as clear as day."

"Lightning strike, huh?" I said, thinking of Old Sassafras.

"Oh no. Nothing like that. Me? I think it gave up."

"The tree?"

"You know," she said impatiently. "Too much

14

dead-on sun. Too much interference. Birds pecking and scratching. Kids cutting at the bark and digging up the roots and sometimes it's easier to throw over and just give it all up. Don't you think?"

I shook my head, tried for lightness, tried for deflection. "What a way to go, I guess." What exactly were we talking about?

"Would you rather . . ." She trailed off.

I waited out her quiet, watched the storm clouds fight across her face.

Still in the circle of my arms, she pushed herself half up. "What if there was a place," she said, "where you would never grow old, never die. All comfort, all ease. A place where nothing ever changed. The perfect life."

I frowned. "Well—"

"But you could never fall in love. Never love and never leave. Never know true love, not ever, not once."

Because I was young. Because I was weak. Because I didn't know what to say, didn't even really know what we were discussing. Because of all this—or maybe none of it—

I laughed. "I mean, it sounds like a bargain, right?"

There was a beat of silence. Then, "Maybe."

She pulled out of my arms and stood. Now that the gutted clouds had spent their load the moon was back, and in its naked light her body looked as slick and smooth as one of her lost sculptures. She stepped over her sodden heap of clothing.

"Maybe," she said again.

Just that.

Before I could pull my own words together in reply, she was gone. Light tickled the far horizon and a couple of predawn birds began clearing the night from their throats, but in the now of this moment, the dark still ruled. Her last word lingered in the space she'd left behind.

In the moonlight, the stone beside me dripped and flowed with liquefied dreams.

———

Impossibly—because hadn't a year passed, hadn't a lifetime?—the bar was still open.

The bartender took in my bedraggled, wet-dog look and poured me a double. "Ah, that girl," he said, shaking his head. "It was bound to happen sooner or later. If she knows what's good for her, she'll get out now. While she still can."

"She told me—" I shook my head once, hard. I sighed.

Night wind blew low through the door I'd left

cracked open. I was the only drinker in the place. Even Old Sass was nowhere in sight.

Finally I said, "The tree. The old beat-up one, couple miles from town. You know it?"

"Sure, who doesn't. Know how it got that way?"

"Tell me." See? I was learning.

"I saw it all go down with my own eyes—that hollow in the center? You're little enough, you can get right inside. And what do you think is up in there? Rot. Barely a shell of bark left holding the whole thing together by now. No idea what from. I got up in it one time, and boy, I got out of there fast. Some bug, some blight, some *thing* infected that great, gorgeous beauty. Got under its skin, you might say. Ate it from the inside out till there was nothing left. Nothing but a dead, empty shell."

I studied the bottom of my glass. I thought about trees. I thought about dark, tumbleweed towns. I thought about a life spent carving in soap, just to watch the next big rainstorm sweep it all away.

The barman laughed. "You know what they say about this place?"

I shook my head, accepted the new pour, gulped it down in one.

"They say you have to be lost in order to find it. Well and truly lost. That's what they say." He flatlined the bottle and tossed it empty into the bin. "Well. We all just slog out our lives here, so what does that tell you?"

My brain hurt. If only the room would stop spinning. "How long have you lived here?" Wherever *here* even was.

He laughed again. "You heard the girl, didn't you? You know what's good for you, you better go."

Permanence. Impermanence. Love. Would you rather?

God help me, I went. I went and I walked and I didn't look back. Propped outside the café door I found my gas can, inexplicably full. I picked it up and started back down the long road toward the Lost Soul.

———

The next thing I knew it was morning and my mouth was hellcotton and I was spread out on my own back seat and the car roof above me was aflame with midday light. My gas gauge was at a comfortable halfway mark, with only a hardscrabbling in the dust outside and a tipped-over jerrycan to show the night before had ever happened.

And looped three times in a loose knot around my wrist, a bloodred cord.

CONFIDENCE GAME

Step 1: Getting to know your Neep.

Congratulations! You are the proud owner of a Neep. To make the most of your new houseguest, please read this booklet carefully from start to finish. Tenebrix Enterprises cannot accept any claims or suits from users who have disregarded or countermanded any of the material outlined herein. Due to their extreme neural plasticity, each Neep will customize and bond in their own unique way. When it comes to your Neep, you are in complete control! Give yourself the best chance for success by adhering fully to the best practices laid out in the following pages.

It was the latest viral sensation: the Neep! Standing about yea high, two sticking-out duck-paddle feet below a furry blob of a body, like a boiled egg in a mink coat. Just the right size to perch on the palm of your hand. Oh, and 50% eyes.

Meet the Neep! Yours to keep! You hear that jingle once, man, you are *not* getting it out of your head. That's the point of advertising, obviously. Doesn't make it any more resistible. I didn't set out to be wooed, I swear I didn't. But don't those social media ads know their market? By the third closeup pan of those slow-blink eyes, I was hook-line-and-sinker hooked.

Did I have any inkling where it all would lead? I wish I could say I did, but I'd be lying. Then again, how much of belief is wanting to believe, is framing reality so fully in mental Portrait Mode that everything else blurs to the backdrop?

So I called the toll-free number, just like in the old days, even though there was probably a souped-up webshop I could've patronized instead. The raspy old-ster took my card info and mailing address and the deed was done. Then I set to stalking my mailbox like an addict anticipating the rush, just knowing this fresh poison's gonna be your new best friend.

I mean, why should the kids get to have all the fun?

———

Doug doesn't get what it's like to grow up poor. It's not like he was born with a silver spoon up his ass or anything. But there's a wary kind of foresight you develop when you live every day never quite sure how—or if—your next meal is getting to your plate. It does get there somehow, it always does; or if it doesn't, you're a kid and you put that day out of your mind in favor of all the other times it did; things'll be better next time, we'll get double helpings tomorrow, every one of us, just see if we don't. You get the drift. I won't say it changes you, that kind of life, because isn't it just the way things are, the way they've always been? But it's not something you can ever really grasp from hearing it told. You either know it, or you don't. That's the truth of it.

Heady thoughts. This was the kind of late-night shit that made me aggressively not a morning person. *Sleepless night again, babe?* Doug would say in a couple of hours, when I dragged myself down the hall toward my office five minutes before stand-up, tripping over the bags under my eyes. And I'd turn up the sides of my mouth and grab the industrial-sized coffee mug he was proffering and hold out my cheek for its peck like the dutiful wife I am.

Portrait Mode: engaged.

———

The box on my front stoop was enormous, all disclaimers: FRAGILE! HANDLE WITH CARE! THIS SIDE UP! Air holes all the way around.

Doug was on early shift all week and already long gone for the day. One thing less to stress about. He's never been one for gimmicks, this man of mine. Meat and potatoes, color inside the lines, first page first and last page last. You know the type. I've found it best to have my whims all sorted and set before he makes their acquaintance. Less fallout to mop up that way.

So me and the box cutter, we got down to business.

Inside: a crate. Sturdy. Wood slats. Stuffed with that natural fiber packing shit that looks like bougie straw. For something the size of a handshake, this little sucker was traveling large.

Not gonna lie, my heart was going full jackhammer by this point.

Out came the crate. Set it on the step behind me. Broke down the box into neat cardboard squares, ready for the dumpster down the street. Breathable packing foam goes direct to the recycler. What is it people say? It's not the dead body that gets you caught, it's the blood spatter pointing the way. What I'm saying is, I had no wish to incriminate myself. Even then, that felt important somehow.

The crate was lidded and sealed, just a hint of fur poking through one of the side slats. Almost there! Now to take this party indoors. The walk upstairs never felt so long. I set the crate on the alpaca rug. Drew the blinds on my manicured yard, as if the koi might leap from their sculpted pond to try and cop a look. Then I dropped into that splay-legged sitting pose my stepma always said would grow me up pigeon toed. Ha! Look at me now, Darla.

Up with the lid. Gently, so gently, push aside the packing fluff.

And there it was. My new obsession.

———

You develop an understanding, when you've been with someone for enough years. I wouldn't say me and Doug see eye to eye on too many things. Not if I'm being truthful. But gradually, you find what works. A my-tea-your-coffee compromise. Give a little, take a little. You find a way to live, don't you? Growing up on the streets, that's the first thing you learn: keep those coping skills sharp, like a knife in your boot. Always ready. Just in case.

You learn to adapt, is what I'm saying.

But. Here's the thing regular folks don't get, even those who are passing self-aware. How it dogs you, the past. How you leave it but you never really lose it. And more: how there will always be some part of you that doesn't fully want to. Some poisonwood shard stuck deep that will always hunger for the gutter. It dies hard, that urge for self-destruction. If it dies at all. So what do you do? You learn to choose your obsessions. You scheme and you scope and you plan and you pick them before they pick you.

Then you fling your goddamn caution to the wind and hope for the fucking best.

By this point, I needed a drink.

I left that Neep half-unpacked and went back downstairs. From the fridge door I grabbed a green smoothie, gave it a good long shake-up, and poured. Wheatgrass, creatine, beet powder. Stir and chug. For good measure, I dropped for twenty-five diamond push-ups. Cursed myself for not making it to thirty. Tomorrow's goal.

Ready? Almost.

Ice-cold shower. Then, the walk-in closet. Today's outfit, fresh from the dry cleaner, on today's hanger. Gold stud earrings. Heavy chain in two loops around my neck. Stockings. Pumps.

Are they high enough, the walls? Will they keep me safe from the darkness inside?

Step 2: Caring for your Neep.

A newly fledged Neep needs its beauty rest! Hatchlings may sleep upward of eighteen hours a day, though this will decrease with time to a standard twelve hours by full maturity. Even during waking periods, a Neep strongly prefers full darkness. Sunshine may be tolerated in moderate doses, however.

Neep benefit from an iron-rich diet. Recommended foods include spinach, kale, raw eggs, nuts, pumpkin seeds, and quinoa. A full list is included at the end of this booklet. For an occasional treat, offer a few dried kidney beans. Be warned: if provided too often, these can dull your Neep's teeth, which causes distress and may result in chewing damage to household objects.

Caution: Under no circumstances should meat or meat products be fed to your Neep. Tenebrix Enterprises disclaims any responsibility for a Neep whose palate has been turned by flesh.

The crate was like a nest, like a little bed. The Neep lay flat out / belly up / eyes shut, its crayon-yellow webbed feet pointing up at the roof. Wide packing ribbons crisscrossed the furry body. One looped each leg to the crate's edge; another cupped the round belly, with its skinny arms tucked near-invisibly under the fluff. A third topped its head. Each ribbon had a tiny snap and came off easily. No budget spared on the trimmings, that was for sure.

What now? Was there an on switch or something?

Wasn't it supposed to, like, move? Blink or something? Surely that wasn't just an advertising gimmick.

I prodded the belly with a fingertip. It gave a little to the touch, like a fuzzy water balloon. Warm, okay. But still as a corpse. I slid my fingers around the head and scooped up that floppy doll body, turned it side to side. No buttons. No wires. Huh.

Upside down. Back upright.

I brought it closer to my face. Nothing.

Had I just exchanged a week in the Bahamas for some purebred organic stuffie?

It wasn't even the money I cared about, though that wasn't nothing. Something else was going through my head. Maybe I said it aloud, to my shame. *I thought maybe this was it. The thing that would save me. Some part of me needed something and I thought you were it and I guess I was wrong, but I wanted you so, so bad.*

Bam.

Eyes sprang open. I nearly dropped the little critter. But I didn't.

The Neep gave one full-body shiver. A current of breath started up.

Three seconds later I held a squirming, wriggling teacup pig of a thing. Suddenly we're all blur, all motion! It was a true two-hand operation to keep from dropping it. Did I mind? Don't make me laugh. Fishhook, meet jaw. Cut me open and pull out my guts. Already there was nothing in the world but those green ocean eyes on mine. That tiny perfect O of a mouth.

It yawned and—holy shit! That's one jagged, anglerfish mouthful right there.

Long-lashed eyes drifted shut. A puff and a very low purr. Nap time already?

I set my Neep back in the crate, smoothed the soft packing material down around it. The little body started to shiver. What could I use? I grabbed my new Hermès birthday scarf. Tucked it in on both sides like a tiny quilt. Perfect.

There was a sticker on the edge of the crate, I saw now. Maybe it had been stuck on the crisscross ribbons, but it had clearly come loose in transit. I pulled it up.

Important! Read full manual before activating device.

My face flushed hot. *Device?* This was my Neep! My living, breathing, purring lifesaver. My treasure.

Still. Instructions were instructions.

I found the booklet under some more packing fluff and sank down on the window seat. Lamp on. Flipped through the glossy pages. There was a whole section on activation. Blah blah *Spoken words of welcome*—ah, so that was what did it!—blah blah *Keep warm*. So clearly ahead of the game here.

The Care and Feeding section was a bit more interesting. Not technically a living creature, the Neep, but not a *thing* either. Some state-of-the-art hybrid, AI and robot-tech mixed with actual living cells. Self-learning brain. Self-healing body. It consumes but does not eliminate: somehow the organic matter is converted into body growth and neural development. Essentially a highly efficient composting machine. I read the pamphlet right to the end, as instructed. Then I shoved it in my nightstand drawer. What a crock of legalistic mumbo jumbo.

And yet, in spite of it all. Here we were! My very own Neep and me.

I leaned down till my face was right against the edge of the crate and whispered: "You are exactly what I wanted. I will keep you and love you forever."

The Neep flutter-puffed its breath. The belly rounded up just a bit more.

Ultimate high.

Step 3: Interacting with your Neep.

Neep are nocturnal, and benefit from a safe enclosure to roam during their waking hours. It is not advisable to release your Neep outdoors at night, or at any time without careful supervision. Tenebrix Enterprises stringently disclaims any responsibility for damages incurred by free-range Neep.

For a peak ownership experience, we recommend a full initial bonding with your Neep. The optimal method of completing the bonding circuit is the sharing of confidences. Neep love to hear you speak. They have no vocal cords, and thus are the ultimate listening partners. Tell them anything and everything: the more you share, the better. Bonded Neep can develop limitless affection for their person. Your Neep will delight in being awakened several times throughout the day for feeding and confidence sharing. Remember: the deeper and more personal the confidences shared, the faster the bond will grow and the stronger the connection will be.

Was there a point in our marriage when Doug and I told each other everything? Well, sure. Though *everything* is such a slippery word. Take a slick new mansion built on reclaimed swampland. You're a contractor, you're a real estate bro looking to close a deal, what story are you gonna tell? Twelve-foot ceilings. One-eighty ocean views. Four-zone heating. Marble countertops. Right? Nobody's gonna pull up a chair and be all, *Let me tell you about the landfill garbage that went into this lot. Let me tell you how deep the bones are buried. Let me tell you how the ocean eats the shore night by night, bite by bite. Let me tell you how fragile is the ground below your feet, should you sign on this dotted line.*

Well. Everything is as everything does, my stepma used to say. Good old Darla. All the best lessons are taught by hard example, aren't they? 'Cause that's the thing about relationships: You don't get a trial run. You don't get to practice. And once that everything ship has sailed, well. That's it then, isn't it?

So, yes. In all the ways that count, it's me and Doug and the truth, best bedfellows, getting it on hot and heavy every night. That's my story and I'm sticking to it.

All of which brought me to now, to this intriguing, potbellied puffer which, apparently, wanted my confidences. Meaning . . . what? Rooting around in my past? Digging up my old shit and serving it up with a side of iron-rich nutrients? After all this time. After all I'd become, how hard I fought for that distance. The idea should have repelled me. It should have horrified me. Instead, I felt strangely . . . hungry. And not just because I was at the local farm store, trawling the aisles and stocking up on dark leafy greens and artisanal salt-free seeds.

I would cook dinner tonight, I decided. How long had it been? Doug would be home early and I'd do the whole Mediterranean spread he used to love. We'd split a bottle of wine. He'd tell me about the day's surgeries. I'd introduce my Neep. Why not? He was going to find out about it anyway. Wasn't he?

On the other hand.

There was the basement. My home gym barely dented the space. No windows, plenty of quiet, a door that locked. Doug hadn't set foot down there in years.

Yeah. Probably a good idea to give the Neep a chance to get settled before doing any introductions. Ease the little guy in slowly. It just made sense.

———

I slept badly that night. Doug was passed out next to me,

on his back with arms flung over his head, all his soft parts wide open. Who sleeps like that? I wondered if my husband had any reclaimed-land skeletons locked inside his head. Somehow, I thought not.

I rolled out of bed. Forget the slippers, skip the robe. There is something bracing about the night chill. The way it starts in your toes and pulls up your legs, goes through you like a charge. It's the best way I know to get back to sleep: Walk the halls a bit. Let the cold dig its teeth in the old scars. Become the darkness.

None of that tonight, though. Back to bed was the last thing on my mind.

I kept the lights off as I crept downstairs. Eased open the basement door. Stepped through. Shut it carefully behind me. Down the staircase. The slice of window let in a quarter-light that carved the shadows and gave them bulk. The crate was empty.

Behind me, a low chirp.

Two eyes, green-glinting in the dark.

I turned. I squatted down. Held out both hands, palms up, low to the floor. A snuffling sound. The green dimmed as the Neep's gaze turned downward, scuffing at the ground. A tickling at the tips of my fingers. He climbed onto my palm, webbed feet scratchy and rough. I brought my flat hand, with its dear cargo, toward my face. The Neep craned back and looked up at me with those mesmerizing eyes.

Slow blink.

"Hello, little guy," I whispered. "What do you want to know? Should I tell you about myself?"

It happened quick. He was perched on my palm. Then he wasn't. Skinny, knobbly joints unfolded. One limb snaked out to hook on my left collarbone. The other snagged the right. His pear body dropped to hang between my breasts, turned half to the side, fuzzy-soft against my bare skin. I undid two buttons and slid my Neep closer against my chest. Redid the buttons, tucked the soft cotton snug around him.

What now? Oh, yes. Confidences.

One beat hovering on some mental brink. It had been so long. So, so long and the walls were so high. But again: that twang of hunger. That very light tug toward release.

I sighed. Pulled off my earrings. Slid all six rings off my fingers. Dropped the lot on the low coffee table. Then I leaned back against the side of the couch. Settled the Neep more comfortably on my chest. And started at the beginning.

As I talked, I watched my chest rise and fall with each breath. Each spoken word. It was almost visible,

how my past slid from my open lips and out into the
open air. Regaining shape. Form. Power?

No. Never that.

Small tufted body to the side, round eyes upturned
toward me, the Neep absorbed it all. I thought maybe
there was a smile on his face.

———

It became a pattern. Each night I'd lie in bed, eyes wide and
fixed on the ceiling. Waiting for Doug's breathing to slow
and stabilize. Sometimes I'd even drift off. But I always
woke. Addiction: the ultimate self-sustaining organism.
Then I would swing my legs to the floor, tiptoe downstairs, curl up with my Neep. He especially loved it when
I hand-fed him raw spinach, holding each long stem while
he nibbled the leaf down to a nub with tiny razor teeth.

Meanwhile I talked. Opened myself wide and let
it all out.

Everything else suffered. Of course it did. My
weight bench grew a film of dust. I missed more work
stand-ups than I made. What did I care? Let my man-
ager report me if he cared to. I had brought in more
contracts that year than the rest of my group com-
bined. My nights were for my Neep; my days spent

awaiting sundown. Sometimes I would cave early in the day, creep downstairs and wake him with a light belly tickle and a handful of seeds. Big eyes blinking wide. Big gaze fixed and adoring. My Neep and me, we'd walk the manicured paths in the backyard. Breadcrumbs for the koi. Sugar water for the hummingbird feeder. Halcyon days.

———

One morning I woke and felt a stirring on my chest. The Neep! I was in my bed but somehow—he was here, still hooked in his favorite spot on my chest. And Doug not a foot away! I rolled fast to the left, though Doug was sound asleep. I tugged the little body, tried to pry him loose. But no go. That little sucker was latched on good.

As if to sweeten the deal, he purred. Big eyes upturned to me.

Well. Why not? Keeping my back to the bed, I hustled across the room and pulled my newest Magnolia Pearl dress off the hanger. The Neep disappeared beneath the roomy folds. My favorite listening buddy: now fully portable.

"Hey, babe," Doug said, stifling a yawn. He pulled out his phone. "Shit, I'm on call."

When he was gone, I pushed a week's worth of worn clothing off the window seat and onto the floor. Kicked my resistance bands out of sight under the bed. I leaned back on the velvet roll pillow. The wind outside gently ruffled the leaves. Orange-spotted koi gently stirred the surface of their pond. The whole world was a smile.

I scratched my Neep's head lightly. "I was just thinking, last night. About the alley. Did I tell you about the alley behind the drugstore? It was one of our favorite places, back in the day . . ."

———

Days passed like this. Weeks. The holidays came and went. January slush. February darkness. My workdays passed in an unseeing blur: I existed in and for my subterranean world. The Neep was butterball round. He'd long outgrown the palm of my hand, but he never tired of hearing my voice. He would listen and listen and listen. There was nothing I couldn't say. After all these years, the exquisite pain of a scar reopened. The free flow of new blood unhindered. And it was all met with the same dark, unwavering gaze. Every blink an acceptance. A taking in.

Imagine this: To just be who you are. Nothing more and nothing less.

It should have lasted.
It could have lasted.
It could never have lasted.

———

Here's the thing about compartmentalization, about boxing and sealing up the past. It's never less than all or nothing. You think you've got it locked away, you think you're safe. And then: something happens. You open a peephole. You let someone in—just a bit. Just a part. What they don't tell you is the moment you let down your guard, that's when you stop being in control. If you're not controlling the story, the story's controlling you. It's out of your hands, after that. Once you pull that first unraveling thread, who can tell what might happen?

Go ask our gal Pandora. She knows how it is.

———

"You were talking in your sleep again last night," Doug said over breakfast one morning. "Who is Darling?"

"Darla," I said automatically. Then bit my tongue. Shit.

He looked up at my tone. One eyebrow up.

I shrugged. "Somebody from my past."

Eyebrows higher. "Which part of your past?"

"Oh. Just a . . . school friend. A girl from . . . fin-ishing school. Nobody important."

Had I looked down as I said that? Did it matter, this small untruth, this edit?

From his hidden spot on my chest, the Neep shifted in place. From inside my collar, the quickest blink of red.

Step 4: Cautions and disclaimers.

It is not advised to introduce a Neep into a household containing pets or small children. If in doubt, a general mass greater than forty pounds for any co-habitant is strongly recommended. Please note that your Neep's growth and size will vary by model. The more closely bonded your Neep, the larger and healthier the final specimen.

One final caution: While in the presence of your Neep, you must only ever speak the full truth. If your Neep is ever exposed to a lie, it will begin to turn. Once this programming is initiated, there is no means of reversal. Tenebrix Enterprises disclaims all responsibility for a turned Neep. We cannot overstate the severity of this warning. Please refer to the full set of disclaimers and waivers signed at the time of purchase for more details and information.

From all of us in the Tenebrix Enterprises family, we wish you the very best as you care for, feed, and bond with your Neep, and a long and happy life.

I woke to a burst of pain. White-hot scoring across both my Achilles tendons. I yelled and sat up, heart pounding. Doug woke with a start and reached for the lamp, but I called, "No!" I quick-patted my chest. No Neep. I relaxed, let myself lean into Doug. Still trembling.

"What's going on?" His eyes were wide in the darkness.

Outside the window, lightning flashed. There was no thunder, not a sound. Just white light slashing the night.

The pain was subsiding. But I could still feel the ghost of it. Real? Or part of a dream? I reached down, touched the back of my ankle, and gasped in pain.

"Are you okay?" Doug was up now. He came around my side of the bed and pulled off the covers, moved my hands and angled his phone light. I turned over so he could examine the spot I'd been touching. He frowned.

"What?"

He clicked a photo, brought it up to show me. There was a raised red line across my tendon. A clean slice, like an old wound that had been torn and stitched and was now nearly healed.

"That looks weeks old," he said. "When did you hurt it?"

I shook my head, searching for words. What could I say? I slapped my forehead. "Oh! Of course. Must have been at the park the other week—you remember, I told you about that twisted fence I tried to climb over."

"I don't remember anything like that."

From the dark of my walk-in closet, two eyes blinked. Flashing red.

Which to save? Who to choose? I pushed on. "Well. You were at work. I'm sure I told you about it that night. Anyway, it was nothing. Just a careless moment." I kept my legs flat against the mattress. Lest Doug see the matching slash on the other tendon.

He persisted, though. Sat down opposite me on the bed. Took both my hands in his and tilted his head to look deep into my eyes. "What's going on with you?" he said. And well he might. It had been weeks, maybe more, since we'd spent any real time together. Over the past months as I'd pulled farther and farther away, he'd gone from oblivious to baffled to hurt. Did it bother me? Not gonna lie: I'd barely cared. If you've ever jumped headlong into the lava pool of obsession, you know what I mean. And if you haven't . . . can you truly say you have lived? Isn't that life, though: the struggle between the safety of the pocket and the razor's edge of feeling fully alive?

Now, though. Now.

His question caught me. What *was* going on? I had long since decided not to tell him about the Neep. It was far too late, and the confidence game only played for two.

I squeezed his hand. Set it gently back down on the bed.

Doug sighed. "We're never going to talk about this, are we." It was a statement rather than a question. I examined it and saw no lie.

New jags of lightning tore at the sky. I got out of bed and walked to the window. Flash: small bones strewn across the ghostly night lawn. Flash: spotted scales and long gut strings smearing the paving stones. Flash: the empty koi pond, still as glass.

———

Do we talk much, Doug and me? I suppose that depends on how you define *talking*. By the next evening, the landscapers had finished their rush repair job—the night's carnage clearly the work of the storm, never mind any question of how lightning might hunger for flesh— and now we sat in our Adirondack chairs, sipping mint juleps and looking out on our empire.

The storm was over. The night had passed. What next?

At the edge of my hearing, a low scuffle. Not unlike the sound of small feet scurrying, scurrying. It had been two days since I'd visited the basement. The door stayed locked on my secrets, yet I knew the real truth. That lock had never been as secure as it seemed. Still, I held the power. Of course I did. And even then, a small voice, whispering, *What if you just . . . told Doug? What if you tried?* Old scars and new pulled and itched. My mouth strained to open.

It's just—sometimes you know someone won't understand. Won't ever get it.

And this: sometimes there is just too much to lose.

Let's say. Let's just say. What if you *did* open your mouth one day? What if you did just . . . put it all out there? What if you were lured in by the mood: the dusk, the air thick with magnolia and cypress, the monarchs fluttering on the edge of your vision . . . the second julep, the third. You open your mouth. And before you know it, everything is out. It's all there: the streets, the fear, the life, the chase, the plunging blade, the moment the moment the moment. It's all out before you think to look up, and then.

And then.

That face opposite you. That awful, beautiful face. It loved you, just moments ago. But now? Now you've gone too far and it's immediately clear this moment is something you can never erase. You can never undo.

Look. Don't be ridiculous. We both know that would never happen.

Must never happen.

———

I wonder if it ever occurred to Pandora.

The box is open. The demons are out. The world awaits plunder.

But. What if—what if that wasn't quite . . . *it?* What if there was a moment before it all went down. A moment between *late* and *too late.* A moment when she could still reach down.

Could feel for the knife hidden in her boot.

———

If there's one thing you learn growing up with nothing, it's how to hold on to what you've got.

———

I wait till the darkest part of the night. I lure it with spinach and seeds. I whisper my love and devotion. I ignore the red the red the red. I bring it to the crate, snug now for the plump, filled-out frame. I tuck my birthday scarf around its body as it lies quiescent, eyes never leaving mine. I bring out my resistance bands, fasten them in place around each of the limbs, around the top of the head.

I close the crate. I add a small bicycle lock. Seal it tight.

The original shipping box is gone. No matter. Outside, I choose the best from my rock garden. Push them through the slats.

The koi pond is deep. It will keep my secrets.

I squint up at the rising moon. There is a hint of spring in the air. I will pick some fresh mint from my garden before I go back inside.

THE TASTE
OF YELLOW

"Would you kill for Jesus?" Nathan asks me late
Sunday night. He's breaking the rules by talking after
lights-out. But we've already scooted side by side in
our top bunk instead of head to toe like we're meant
to, so I guess that's the slippery slope of sin for you
right there.

"Jesus wouldn't tell us to kill," I answer, because part
of being a brother is knowing everything.

"Moses then," Nathan says.

"Moses is dead."

We keep our voices low. Through the shed walls we
can hear the adults talking around the campfire, singing

a bit. Someone reading aloud. It's enough to make the littles toss and turn, restless in their bunks—SuEllen and Hannah are light sleepers. We shouldn't add to the noise. But Nathan loves bickering as much as he loves our bedtime spoonful, and that's saying something. I can still taste the sweet honey on my lips and we're both drifting, happy-drowsy. But I'm big enough now it won't put me to sleep like it does the others. Even Nathan will be out soon. For now, he drones on.

"Who then? Everybody has someone they'd kill for. Who's yours, Sol?"

Sometimes I can't tell if my twin brother is the smartest or the stupidest person I know. The answer to his question is obvious. I know it and he knows it. And he knows I know it. At least, I think so. Anyhow, I'm not giving him the satisfaction.

"Be still, heathen," I say instead.

Nathan snickers. The kerosene heater's only just off, so it's hot as the Lake of Fire up here. We kick down the sheet and roll back-to-back. Our spine-seams zip together like they did in the womb. Or so Mari said when she saw us like this once. Though I'm not sure how she'd know since we were on her inside and that's not a where you can actually see. I don't care. All that matters to me is this is what safety feels like.

My mind is drifting, but my brother's voice pulls me back.

"Sister Jerusha," he says. "That's who it is for me."

Then he rolls over and goes to sleep, as if the world has not pinholed, as if it has not narrowed to one hard point of yellow light.

———

Brother Rob talks about a Road to Damascus experience, like the Apostle Paul had, when the scales fall off your eyes and everything around you goes sharp and clear. What I do not do in this moment: Sit up so fast I hit my head on the tin roof. Scream out loud. Shake my brother so he spills out all the details. What I do in this moment: Lie very, very still. Eyes round. Breath coming in small calf pants.

I will never sleep again.

———

We don't celebrate birthdays since coming to the Farm-stead. The first few years here, Mari would slip us an extra carob-honey oatmeal ball on our day to show she remembered. But that didn't last. This year she's gone the opposite direction. I would think she forgot our birthday altogether except there is so much purpose to her show of not remembering: the closer the day, the tighter her lips, the stiffer her back. Two nights ago she shut herself in the vision tent. I haven't seen her since.

Tomorrow we turn twelve. Tomorrow night is Mad Night.

"One of God's little miracles of timing," said Brother Rob.

"Adults at last," said Sister Jerusha.

Mari was already pulling the heavy tent flap shut behind her, disappearing.

———

I get up before dawn, hang off the side of our triple bunk, and drop to my toes. The cold cement starts me full-on shivering. I wish I'd pulled the cover back over Nathan. This high up the Blue Ridge, summer is more an idea than a truth. Tough living makes the living tough, or so says Brother Mark. All I know is sweaters aren't allowed till October, and if you actually believe going barefoot is optional, then you're following the letter of the law and not the spirit. I sling my forager's pouch across my shoulders. My headlamp hangs loose around my neck.

Outside, I stop by the still-smoldering fire. Empty mason jars scatter the ground among the camp chairs and sitting stumps. I gather the sticky jars and line them up on the trestle table. One goes in my bag. Then I set out for the hives.

It's cold. And gets colder the more I climb. Every few minutes I fist my hands and clench my chest muscles. This gives a little burst of warmth and keeps off the shivers. "Be strong and of good courage," I tell myself. The hives are waiting.

———

I am not ready for this day. I am not ready.

The day has chosen me and I am not prepared.

———

The Farmstead is big on two things: God's Word and mad honey. Feed your soul and feed your body, so says Brother Rob at least once a week during our school sessions. It doesn't take much to turn him from math to what he likes to call a history lesson. He's not wrong: it is the history of the Farmstead, the history of us. Brother Rob is the one who started the commune, ten years ago. He likes to say he isn't the head over anyone, but I don't see others leading meetings or choosing which Scriptures to read for Vespers. And then there's the bees. That was all Brother Rob's doing. He spent years backpacking through Asia, and that's where he first learned about hallucinogenic honey.

Bees make honey, right? They gather the nectar from the flowers around their hive. But in some places, the flowers around are all poisonous. Human-poisonous, not bee-poisonous. Especially certain rhododendrons. And when bees get busy with just those plants, their honey takes on all kinds of weird and mystical proper-ties. It's an ancient tradition, finding and harvesting mad honey. Get Brother Rob in a good mood and he'll talk about the nomads who roam the mountains in Turkey, scaling cliff faces to reach the honeycomb deep in the rocks. Bees half the size of your fist, so says Brother Rob, and just like he tells it I can see it: you're digging into the crevices with your bamboo pole and the bees come boiling up and it's all you can do not to slide off your rope ladder and crash to the depths below. Some people have, I guess. But Brother Rob didn't. He made it back and he brought all that knowledge with him.

Special honey for a special people. A chosen people. He started the Farmstead way up here in the mountains—not quite the ideal environment for cultivating mad honey, he says, but the best he could get. Brother Rob taught Sister Jerusha how to care for the bees, how to keep the right balance of rhododendron to other pollinating flowers, how to tell from the color when the honey is just mad enough to harvest. The compounds build up over time. You want your honey strong but not too strong. Not deadly.

All of this he taught Jerusha, and Jerusha taught me.

———

At the cliff base I switch on my lamp. Dawn is pushing back against the night, trying to break through. And it will. Soon. But meanwhile, I've got climbing to do.

So, here: my finger of yellow light points the way and I follow.

I'm panting as I pull myself up over the last boulder. My toes have that uneven feeling I hate, half stiff with cold and half pulsing hot from the effort. I stamp them on the packed dirt so the blood flows evenly again. Then I unwind the rope from my waist and lift my gaze to the heavens. The early climb was worth it: I hit Bee Cove just as the sun breaks over the far trees, and *bam*, the night goes. Yellow. It's all yellow and gold: the world, the trees, the down-mountain below. The Farmstead, too, though that's fully hidden from sight. My feet settle in a patch of sun and my hands unclench and I can feel God. God is the sun and God is the sky and God is the buzzing in the hives behind me.

My reason. My purpose. My bees.

"Good morning, you lovelies," I whisper. They're tiny and I'm not sure they have brains, not real ones like us who are made in God's image. But I know they can hear the love in my voice.

I've been Sister Jerusha's assistant for one year, two months, and twenty-three days. Someone started calling me the Little Beekeeper that first week, and the name stuck. I sure was little when I started coming up here, thin as a bulrush sprout and barely higher. But that didn't last. This time last year, I stopped being a child. That's the way of nature, the way of the world. Isn't it? Everything grows into its purpose.

So said Sister Jerusha, anyhow. I had no cause not to believe her. I had no cause not to let her do the things she did.

Nowadays I'm well gone from little, and boy do I look it. Especially next to Nathan. Mari says I sucked half the life out of him in the womb. I don't know about that, but I do know this: I came into this world feet first, head after, left hand last. My fist closed around my brother's foot. Like I could pull him with me to safety. That's how we came out of our mam and that's how it's been. I look out for him, no matter what it takes. No matter what.

Isn't that what a brother does?

You can't change the past, not one bit of it. I know that. But the future . . .

It wasn't long after I started at Bee Cove that I understood what needed doing. Once I did, it was all so clear: My purpose. My plan. Every moment since then has just been one slow step after another and another. Waiting for the moment, for the call. It's been hard going sometimes. It's harder still if I let my mind wander into that dark-gray up-ahead. Proverbs says that what a man thinks inside his heart, that's who he is. Your thoughts become you.

But if I don't think a thought, then it can't be part of me, can it?

I think about bees. I think about yellow.

———

Today is weeding day at the Cove. I don't have to consult my list anymore for the ratio of *Rhododendron ponticum* to nonpoisonous flowers, what to weed and what to prune and what to leave alone. I know it all by heart now. But it still brings me God's joy to behold.

Of all the wild-scattered blooms, butterfly weed is my favorite. The bees love it. But we can't have too much flowering at once or the honey's balance will be off. It's the mad we're chasing, after all.

I tug up a large plant and toss it from the ledge. It spills orange down the cliffside. I imagine it landing on a patch of fertile soil. I imagine it finding the perfect place to die and decompose and rise again someday, in safety. Somewhere it can grow tall and live on without fear of uprooting.

Here's a patch of oleander. I pull that up too. The pollen is dead poisonous, but it's got no actual nectar. So: entirely useless to the bees. I yank off the pollen-studded flowers, stuff them in my pocket next to the rhododendron I filched on the way up. Waste not, want not.

There's a shuffling behind me. I can't keep my shoulders from clenching. But I don't turn. My hands are caked with soil; the shaking is hardly noticeable. I rub them hard on the legs of my jeans.

"Solomon," she says.

"Sister Jerusha," I mumble. She steps closer, stretches a hand toward me. I scoot away. Jackrabbit steps. No.

I make myself stop, make my back a steel rod. I push down the hot coal in my gut. Standing this straight, our eyes are on a level.

"You're here early again. Already done with your work?"

She doesn't say it looks good, and I wouldn't want her to. I just hold her gaze in silence. Maybe she sees something of my thoughts because she finally looks away. I am still rubbing. All this dirt on my hands, it's caked in too deep. The webs of my palms are black as sin.

"Your hive settling okay?" she asks.

"I was just going up to check now."

She nods and leans heavily on her hip. I wonder how much longer she'll be able to make this climb. I wonder who will become lead beekeeper when she can't any longer. I make myself stop wondering. I think of yellow.

She limps to the hive and peers inside. "Good capping," she says. "Getting close now."

Mad honey has been around for centuries. Back in historical times, there are stories of armies who used it to put their enemies in a stupor and then *bam*, the battle about wins itself, doesn't it? In tiny amounts, there's all kinds of health benefits. A bit more and— so says Brother Rob—you can touch the face of God.

But watch out for your concentration, or you'll be doing that literally. It's all about the dosage. Which is where Sister Jerusha comes in. Brother Rob taught her about the bees, but she's the one who perfected the mad honey.

In her past life, she spent years working in a chemical lab. She taught me all about the grayanotoxins that the bees gather from the deadly *Rhododendron ponticum*. The chemicals go into the honey and give it its *mad* quality. Done right, the end result is a perfect balance: a bit of hallucinogen, a bit of aphrodisiac, a bit of lowered inhibitions. Stir some of it into the mulled moonshine Brother Mark cooks up behind his old trailer, and you've got the perfect recipe for Mad Night.

You've got the Farmstead.

The mad honey is what brought Mari here, and most of the others, too. You'd think that would make Sister Jerusha the leader but no, she's just the beekeeper. I wonder if she's ever thought of that, how much power she actually has.

"I should go up," I say.

She nods. "Check on your color. You keeping an eye on the plant ratio?"

I don't even need to answer that. I turn toward the rocks.

"Don't take the comb out yet," she reminds me. "I know you're eager to show what you've done. But they're still settling in their new spot. If you take it all out too early—"

"The hive will die. I know."

"Go on," she says.

I do, but not because she said so.

As I climb, I think of Ecclesiastes 3. One of my favorite Bible passages: *To everything there is a season, and a time to every purpose under heaven.*

When you split a hive, you gotta move it so slowly. Just a few feet at a time.

A time to be born, and a time to die.

Wait a few days. Then move it again.

A time to plant, and a time to pluck up that which is planted.

It takes an age. But you do it right, you can transport your split-off hive into a whole different space. You can create your own new reality.

A time to heal, and a time to kill.

I brought my bees clear up the cliffside. No rope. No ladder. Just the bare stone, slick with survival moss and cut jagged by the elements. And me.

A time to laugh, and a time to weep; a time to dance, and a time to mourn.

Here on this high ledge, I made my own cove for my own hive. Here, I create my own ratio. Find my own balance. Touch the face of God? I close my eyes and breathe yellow.

A time to get, and a time to lose; a time to keep, and a time to cast away.

It takes time, all of this. But time is something I no longer have. Road to Damascus, there you go. I am not ready. But the day is here.

God shall judge the righteous and the wicked: for there is a time there for every purpose and for every work.

So. I face the hive and I wait. My bees slip out one by one. They circle me. I close my eyes and let them settle. One on my eyelid. Another on my chin. I feel the air stir as each in turn goes about landing, buzzing, rising, landing again.

Would they hurt me if they knew?

"I am sorry," I whisper. I know how it feels to be the pawn in someone else's game.

From the bushes, I pull out my trusty honey bucket. From my pouch, the empty mason jar.

I turn to the hive. I do what needs to be done.

———

When I get back down to the main compound, I see Nathan right away. He's bouncing on his toes, eyes bright and hands opening and closing.

"Where were you? That took forever. I didn't even hear you go! How are the bees? You saw Sister Jerusha?"

My brother and his morning crazies. I shoulder past him toward the shed, but he scurries beside me in little bouncing hops.

"You're so lucky, Sol. What's it like up there? Did she say anything? Did you know that Sister Jerusha—"

"Nathan," I say. "Stop."

He goes still. "What? Did something happen? Is she okay?"

"Jesus wept, Nathan. Why are you so—" I bite off the words. "Jerusha is fine. Just busy."

"Is she bringing the mad honey? For tonight? You're excited, aren't you, Sol?"

I stare him down. "It's not that different from our spoonful, you know. It's basically the same thing."

"It's not the same at all. That bedtime stuff is for babies. This is Mad Night! We get to be there with the adults. In the *barn*. We get to find out what goes on. Just like we always used to talk about."

"I gotta go," I say, pulling the full jar out of my forager's sack. "Gotta take this on over."

Nathan's eyes go round. "Whoa. That batch is *dark*. Must be extra strong. Can I try some? Just a bit."

"Go play with SuEllen, Nath." I turn from the look on his face and I walk away and leave him, because part of being a brother is doing what needs to be done.

I carry my jar toward the barn.

———

We still have to get the littles down to sleep before we join the rest of the adults. Nathan is yawning behind his hand when he thinks I'm not looking. I am thinking slow, sticky thoughts. I am not thinking. I am yellow.

"I'll tuck them in and do the night Scriptures," I tell him. "You go put the bedtime bowl back in the kitchen." I hand it to him, dregs and half-coated spoon and all. This honey is golden. Nathan's right. This is early stuff, barely any grayanotoxins. Just enough to get the littles buzzy and sleepy, so the grown-ups can pass their nights in peace. We still give them just a half-spoonful each, though. Any more and they'll be way past dozy. They'll be sleeping like Abimelech.

Nathan snatches the bowl from me.

"Come back quick," I say. "Let's lie in our bunk a

bit before we go to the barn, till the littles are fully set-tled. You know the adults hate it when they wake up and come crying in the middle of Mad Night."

Nathan snorts because we both know that so well. He scurries from the shed holding the bowl. I start the littles on Psalm 19.

———

Later, I turn in my bunk. Next to me, Nathan's eyes are shut and his sticky lips puff out small bursts of air. There wasn't much left in the bowl I sent back, but looks like it was enough for a good long sleep. It sure kicked in fast.

"You think a plant can ever be more than its roots?" I say. Sometimes it's easier to talk when you know no one can hear. Still, I keep my voice low. "Do you think Ecclesiastes is right? That sometimes there's nothing left but to tear it all down? Start over?"

Nathan doesn't stir. I poke him in the shoulder, just to be sure. Poke again. He flings his arms out and rolls over to face the wall. I push back into his spine-seam. Let the feeling of safety fill me up.

He is sleeping. He is safe.

Still, I make myself count to a hundred, just to be sure. Then I shinny down the bunk and drop noiseless to the floor. Outside, the star-bright sky is penned in by tall pines. The barn is a hive of music and noise and high-pitched laughter. Someone is playing a ukulele.

I take the long way in, through the farmhouse and the summer kitchen. All empty. Mad Nights aren't compulsory, but who'd want to miss one? It's not like there's much else to do around here. It's the reason most folks chose this life, anyhow. The chosen ones. And *oh*. That thought nearly drops me, just that: the chosen are the ones who chose this as their path, aren't they? But what if you're just the pawn on someone else's board?

What if you never got to choose?

The music envelops me as I walk through the patio to the wide-open barn doors. It's barely gone nine. Way early for Mad Night. But it's clear the moonshine has been circulating for a while already. The regular stuff, that is. The mad mix pours out later. That's the point the night is building to. That's the pinnacle.

I don't have to keep my feet moving forward. They do that on their own.

And what is this in the end but a choosing, my choosing this, here, now, at last?

As I cross the threshold, my arm hairs lift and a shiver clips the back of my neck. But it's just the big ceiling fan beating at the night air. There's no open fire, not on Mad Night. The lanterns are all in safe spots. Cushions and pillows and throw blankets everywhere. Lamps on and music sliding out of speakers covered by crocheted afghans. It's the one night the solar-powered generator goes on, but there's no need to be showy about it. High above it all the bare rafters are strung with yellow lights, like rows of hungry eyes watching and watching.

On so many Mad Nights Nathan and I would lie awake, listening to the music and the shrieking laughter, the grunts and the other odd noises we never could quite pin down. Wishing we could see. Wishing we could know. Unlike my brother, though, I have never stopped at wishing. There's a fist-sized crack in the rear wall of the barn that's just the right height for a boy of eleven or so to stretch on his tiptoes and see full inside. You can learn a lot on late nights when the moon's gone dark and you are caught between the sleep of the innocent and the bare truth of the chosen. But that's the way of nature, isn't it?

So: I'm not surprised now to see that the adults have their clothes off already. They're wandering around, snacking and swilling mugs of Brother Mark's finest. Some are dancing a bit, their front parts dangling and swaying. Some are sitting around talking. That's one thing I can never figure, how it feels sitting when you're all bare down below. Isn't it uncomfortable? And also gross? Maybe the moonshine helps. And the mad honey brew, of course. But that's still simmering in the Crockpot.

"Solomon!" Brother Rob has spotted me. He comes over to put his hands on my shoulders. "The littles are down?" When I nod, he squeezes, then pats my back. He frowns as his hand connects with my T-shirt, and I can see him considering my fully dressed state. Then he waves a hand. "Your first Mad Night, eh? Let's take it easy on you. Make your way around a bit. Get to know how the adult fellowship works. There's always next week to get your heart going in the right direction."

"Sir." I duck my head.

"Good man. Now come all the way on in. You've earned it."

He waves a hand toward the low table that's piled with breads and salads, and the stand holding the enormous slow cooker with its curls of steam rising from the top.

"Go," he says. "Go feast up. We'll have dancing in a bit. By the way, where's that brother of yours?"

"Oh. He—well, I think he fell asleep already. He was pretty tired."

Brother Rob chuckles and nods. "Mari's still in the vision tent. But don't worry." He winks, tipping his chin at the Crockpot. "We sent a pitcher in to her." Then he reaches for Sister Sharon, cups the back of her neck and leans in close as she falls toward him in return.

I turn and grab a slice of walnut bread, spread it thick with butter so it looks like a tiny frosted cake. There's a few loose walnuts on the serving plate and I poke them into the butter in a zigzag pattern, bugs on a buttery yellow log. I gobble the slice in two perfect bites.

There's a whoosh behind me and Sister Jerusha looms up. I brush the crumbs off my hands and move away fast. I cross the room and lean over the Crockpot. The liquid inside ripples honey-dark in the lamplight.

Throbbing music pulses behind me. The twinkle lights gleam overhead. I close my eyes and fill my mind with yellow. I can't say if God is or isn't here. I mean, I know God is everywhere. But is He looking down at me now with stern disapproval, one holy finger outstretched as though He might still intervene? Or is He maybe a part of me too, part of my pruning hands, part of this moment, this night where I become a man at last, where I choose my own path?

A time for everything. Alpha and omega.

I turn, so my body blocks the Crockpot from the rest of the room, and lift the heavy glass lid. From my pocket I pull the fistful of crushed pollen and dried-out petals and leaves I gathered this morning. Waste not, want not. Are they needed? I already stirred in my own dark honey, the whole full jar. Is that enough on its own? I think of Brother Rob bringing Mari a pitcher and my chest pinches tight. But you can't stop a hive in motion.

A time for uprooting. I splay my fingers wide. *Bam*.

I pick up the hand-carved wooden spoon and stir until the crushed plants soften and sink into the mix. In this dim light, the surface is murky and indistinct. Just like any other night. On the floor my empty mason jar lies where I left it, half under the table, dregs of black honey still clotting its base. I kick it out of sight. After a moment, I angle the lamp up toward the ceiling.

Then I resettle the lid on the Crockpot and find a spot on the edge of the revels. I keep my gaze fixed on the brew. Curls of steam rise from the pot where it squats like the ark of the covenant on its pedestal. My insides pound. Surely anyone could look at me and *know*. But brothers and sisters drift by in giddy fellowship, some making bits of conversation, some hoping to welcome me in the way of adults on Mad Night. I prop up my smile and keep to my silent vigil. It will soon be time for the moonshine.

It will soon be time.

——

Brother Rob falls first. He looks down at his hand as his fingers open, releasing the drink he was holding. The mug hits a cushion, so it doesn't break, just rolls empty off and down across the floor. The man tips in slow, hairy motion, his limbs rigid, his member suddenly flat. His mouth opens and closes like a river fish. Sister Sharon is moving toward him when she doubles over. She starts vomiting right where she stands, gray bile spilling out and running down her bare stomach. Brother Mark is convulsing. A rank smell fills the room.

I make myself stay still and look straight ahead. It is the least I can do.

I don't realize that Jerusha is still standing until she is in front of me, her wild hair matted with filth. She's holding a mug of moonshine—her second or third, from what I saw—and she sets it down to rush me. She grabs at my T-shirt with both hands.

"What have you done? Solomon! What did you do?"

"You and Nathan," I begin. I shake my head. "I won't let you do it. Not again." I swallow. How is it that of all the moments across the whole of this day, this one right now is the hardest? "My brother," I say finally, "is a child."

Her body is shaking and she falls to her knees, but her eyes are dark and scornful. "And you?"

"I didn't get to stay one for long. Did I?"

Her mouth twists. "He came by tonight, you know. Did you think you could keep him safe? He came to see me earlier. He came and he stayed awhile and then he left." She's tilted over now, nearly flat. "He left with a mug."

She dies in front of me with one arm flung over her head, finger pointing to the nearly full mug of moonshine at my feet.

———

I am numb.

I think about Samson, slaying his enemies with the jawbone of an ass, or Elisha, who smote the Syrian army with blindness before they could attack. I wonder if they were all enemies, every one of those who were killed. I think about roots and plants and things that grow from plants, and how do you know when to prune and when to uproot, and who gets to make that choice? And how do you live with yourself when you do? I think of Mari. Did she ever find her vision?

I do not think of Nathan. I cannot let myself think of Nathan.

That's the thing about choice, isn't it? After all's said

and done, there's no one else to bear the consequences. In the end, it's just you and the road. The road you chose.

I reach down and pick up the mug. I lift it toward my lips.

Then from outside, a sound. I can tell right away, it's Hannah waking from a nightmare. She'll have SuEllen up in no time, and then all of them will be crying. The littles.

I look at the drink in my hands. I look up. Ahead of me, a pool of yellow light.

Holding the mug, I slowly stand.

OVA

She would tell us later she knew immediately that he was gone, knew it from the moment she saw his empty, unslept-in side of the bed, knew it like a dagger gone straight through her heart. That was the way she liked to tell stories, Viv: a bit of drama, a bit of bravado, a bit of embellishment. We all knew this about her. We put up with it because, well, she was Viv, wasn't she? She was all that and more, and we loved her for it.

So there she was, at two-oh-something in the morning. She rolled over and Asshole's side of the bed was empty.

Asshole's side of the bed was never empty.

Viv would not tell you that. She would fill your ears with the sappy story of how they met (county fair, random Ferris wheel pairing, cotton candy, fireworks, sound of listeners gagging). She would tell you the good things about him (always let her choose the pizza toppings, excellent taste in music, knew his way around an engine). She might even go into some detail about him knowing his way around a fuck, though that's not the way she'd put it, oh no, not Viv. She was strangely soft about sex—which might be the only real point in Asshole's favor, that this softness survived him, that despite everything, this was one side of her he couldn't kill.

Until he up and left.

And no, she didn't know it, not immediately and not for a bit after. She just looked over, blinking a few times in the dishwater moonlight that slid through the half-open curtains.

"Asshole?" Viv said. No, she did not actually call him Asshole, but goddamn if we're gonna start using his name now. Grant us this one indulgence.

She could see clearly enough that he wasn't there, but just to be sure she reached over—god's truth, this is what she reported back to us, gushing with tears and snot—and patted his cold, empty side of the bed.

Okay, his side of the bed *was* empty sometimes.

The guy did hold a job. (We'll give him that much credit. Only just, though.) But if he was home, chances are he was in bed. That was where he watched TV, where he received his meals, where he drank his beer. That was where he made long, ranting phone calls to some buddy who didn't seem to be much more than a receptacle for Asshole's nonstop venting and complaints. (Is there a 1-800 number that will endlessly listen to you drone on about nothing? If so, maybe Asshole had found it.) Viv would insist that he got up for bathroom runs, but we're not discounting her ability to put a good face on a crap deal. Literally.

So that night she patted the bare bed and she whispered his name and could this be the moment when she truly started to wonder?

She got up. She turned on every light in the house. She opened the front door.

It's possible that real life did not, does not, happen quite so neatly in tidy sets of three, but cut us a little slack here, won't you? It takes effort to craft a tellable story, even with our luminous Viv thrown into the mix.

So she stared out at the driveway, took four or five steps in her bare feet and pale nightshirt, took in the empty spot by her orange Prius where his pickup used to be. She turned back to the living room and saw the flat patch of gray shag carpet where an elaborate sound system had stood, just hours before. But most telling of all was when she walked into the kitchen and saw that his beer stein—a hand-painted German monstrosity that one of us may or may not have used as a pee jar once in a very dire emergency, true story—was gone. He valued that stein more than his life, Asshole liked to joke. Or more than hers, at any rate. (He never actually said that last bit out loud. He didn't have to.)

Viv knew it had been sitting on the counter right next to the sink. She knew because he'd drunk from it after dinner, and she'd brought it down from the bedroom and had set it right there. She hadn't done the dishes before going to bed like she normally did, but she'd pushed the stein back from the edge for safekeeping.

Now it was gone, clear gone. And only one pair of hands could have taken it.

And that—*that*, not the empty-bed moment, whatever she might say—was when Viv really and truly knew: her asshole boyfriend was gone and he wasn't coming back.

———

When did she first find the growth? Now we're getting to the nub of things. Now the real story begins.

There she was in her empty room, lying flat on her back in a bed that was suddenly twice as big and twice as cold as ever before. Her gaze was fixed on the ceiling and she must have been in some kind of shock. She'd called his number by then, left a voicemail or two, maybe even texted his mom to be sure that she was reading the fortune cookie right. (No, his mom wouldn't have texted back. There's a reason he grew up to be known as Asshole.)

And that was when she found it: a lump.

Did she see it first or did she feel it? We imagine the former. She's that thin, Viv is, barely a bone frame with just enough meat to hold it all together. She never was one for excesses, aside from maybe her storytelling. But in the flesh? She's a paper doll.

So. Flat on her back in a pool of bloodred bedding (we swear we're not making this up; we never did figure out if that was Viv's kinky pleasure or Asshole's, but what a picture she paints, even now, even at her lowest point) and she flung her sheets and stretched her arms and splayed her legs wide because—despite the temperature drop in the bed, in the room, from its missing occupant—the truth was that Viv was suddenly burning up. She could feel it welling in her, rising like a bed of coals from her deepest core. Her whole body pulsed with a growing, raging heat.

Her nightshirt cut off above her waist, and it rode up a bit in any case since she was lying down. The bones of her pelvis jutted high from the bowl of her lower body.

And there it was. Somewhere in the flat, creamy no-man's-land between her shirt's hem and the waistband of her green cotton underwear . . .

A hard, round knob.

———

It was so small at first, she said. Nothing to get riled up about.

Look. There's resilience, we get that. There's taking things in stride.

There's also a time for brisk action and when is it, how is it a body loses that? That capacity for alarm, for movement? For escape?

No, it was not fucking small. And it was not fucking normal.

———

Viv explored the protrusion with careful fingers. She probed all the way around the lump, gently tugged at the tight skin that enveloped it. She pressed her flat palm to the top and the mass gave way—uncomfortably. It was not stiff, but it did not exactly yield, either. The moment she raised her hand, the growth sprang right back.

Already it stood out, fully separate from her body; already it owned its own space. At this point, of course, any number of medical possibilities spring to mind fully formed—not unlike our ovoid arrival—and fight for consideration. A tumor? An abscess? A cyst? Surely one or all of the above.

And yet.

Shouldn't there have been a gradual swelling, a slow inexorable build—seed, cherry, lime—to bring it to its current size? And Viv. The host, you might say. She would have noticed this happening. She just would have. Yet it didn't and she didn't and now here it was and anyone, literally anyone, can tell you that arguing with a fact is a fool's pastime. (Even now, even at this early stage, something is bugging us. It takes a minute to land, but then—where is the bravado? Where is the embellishment? Where is the high drama? Where is the *viv* in our Viv? Though we're a little worried at this point, we know enough to keep it to ourselves.)

So lying in her bed, right there in that life-altering moment, what did Viv think? What did she do?

Viv squeezed her eyes shut. She rolled to her side so the lump rested on the sheets, one lopsided edge almost, *almost* seeming to point directly at the empty side of the bed opposite her. She closed her eyes and . . . what else?

She went back to sleep.

———

If you want to know whether it's typical of Viv to make this type of shattering—or, okay, let's at least say *alarming*—discovery, and then roll over and call it a night? Well, yes. Yes, it is. And maybe if we'd spent the last six years shacked up with Asshole, maybe we too would feel so brim-full of stark reality that at some point we'd be ready to shut it all out. You see what we're saying? Ready to take whatever comes, accept what life delivers, then close our eyes and just hope the whole world goes the fuck away.

It will look better in the morning, right? It always looks better in the morning.

———

Viv's lump did not look better in the morning.

She woke late, groggy, still blazing out heat and so

parched she thought her head might combust on the spot. She rolled out of bed, hit the hardwood on all fours, hunched her way to the bathroom, and downed six cups of water in quick succession. Only then did she remember to look down. She was semiupright now, neck bent, head heavy. One shaking hand braced her weight against the sink while the other gripped the faucet, and of course her belly was fairly distended by that half gallon of water she'd just chugged into it.

Eyes shut. Eyes open. Down went her gaze, down down down.

Yep. There it was: the lump. Fuller, rounder, undeniably bigger than last night. Had it also moved a little to the left? Viv couldn't tell for sure.

She reached down and cupped her palm, spread her fingers to wrap fully around it.

It fit her hand perfectly.

———

This is the point where the story gets a little squirrelly. Let's say you're checking out your body, like any good human should from time to time. Self-care, physical upkeep, all that. And you find a lump. It's not unheard of. Honestly? It's not even rare. So what do you do? You get yourself to the fucking doctor. You get a fucking X-ray, maybe a CT scan, maybe an MRI. Whatever. You do stuff.

Viv would tell you she *knew*, that's why she did what she did, didn't do what she didn't do. She would tell you she knew from the very first moment she laid eyes on it, laid hands on it. Knew that it was something different. Something *other*. Something she wouldn't find help for in any office, doctor's or otherwise.

She always was one for the golden hindsight, that Viv.

Well, she's the protagonist. She gets to call those kinds of shots.

———

So, what did Viv do next? She drank one more cup of water. Then she went right back to bed. She plumped all four pillows up to the headrest so she could lean back against them, a queen on her bloodred throne. She pushed a throw pillow under her hips, so she could see what was going on. She pulled her nightshirt over her head and flung it across the room, because by this point it was just a nuisance.

The lump was still there—but no longer *there*, if you get the drift. The blob was on the move. It now rested just below her belly button. Grapefruit-sized by this point and still resolutely, obscenely round. She touched it with a fingertip, drew concentric circles around and around and around, shivering at the prickling on her taut-pulled skin.

One other thing: it hurt.

Oh, we forgot to mention that, did we? Goddamn, it hurt. The hours ground on, and Viv felt every bloody inch of progress as the lump moved down and through her body. This was no pregnancy, no embryo-to-fetus taking nine months to make its own space, grow and glow, that whole prenatal bonding shit. No, this was fast, violent, take-it-by-force, a commando raid from the inside.

So. What else could she do? She leaned back on her throne and she thrust her hips up and she speared her gaze on the lump as it moved, as it inched, as it carved its way visibly downward.

Did she moan? Did she scream? Did she grind the sheets in her sweaty palms, leaving fingernail gouges in the worn fabric? She'd never confess to it if she had. Pride trumps drama, in the end, doesn't it?

———

On the bright side, she wasn't thinking about Asshole any longer.

From what we could gather, this phase lasted all the rest of that day. Maybe longer. She glossed over this whole part in the telling, Viv did.

Well. Can you really blame her?

But the inevitable has to happen eventually, as the inevitable will.

Viv's pain was still mounting, pressure rising building burning like a star going for supernova. At some point she reached a hand down and yanked off her old cotton underwear—would have torn them all the way off, honestly, if she could have humanly done so—that's how visceral her need was to clear that final barrier, to give herself, give *it*, the space to do what had to be done. (What we're saying is: Viv was not in her right mind. And not one of us can fucking blame her.)

Can you see her there on that bed? Can you?

She is half reclining, propped against her pillows, head flung back so her crown pushes into the wall and her chin is a cliff's edge that plunges the bare length of her torso and down and down. The lump itself is a coal, is a furnace lighting her body on fire—pain and heat and want and the hard round push of something that must. That must *go*. Viv brings both hands down and cups her lowest pelvic region, two hands splaying wide like two wings playing guard to this weird, fragile—

—what? What is she guiding? What is she guarding? Viv is not asking. She's too far gone for that.

She is a rage of heat, she is slick with sweat, her skin is as wet inside as out and she thinks, Go. She thinks, Be. She thinks, Out. Out. Out.

And then it *is* out: There's a gush (and some distant part of her, what used to be the practical voice in her head, once upon a long time ago, whispering *Oh fuck my bedding*) and then. And then it's done.

It's done.

——————

For a while, that was it. Viv glossed over this part, too, but we took note of the missing hours in her story, we see things, we're sharp. Finally she came to, roused a bit, found that she felt less feverish, felt more herself.

Still she lay on the bed, tangled in her mess of sheets. By this point, she wasn't worried—wasn't thinking—about much of anything, really. Anything but the hard, smooth ovoid that fit right between her thighs, and—did you know? How human flesh is so supple as to give when it has to, how it can make within itself just the right amount of space, just the hollow required to fit the need?

Viv bent her knees and tucked her feet and hooked

her ankles behind her. She curled her body into its new shape. And she slept.

———

Eventually, she woke. She woke and she uncurled and she unhooked and she untucked. She lurched out of bed and got down to business. First, a shower. Then to the kitchen, where she opened the fridge and swept everything into a cooler, dumped the contents of the ice maker over top, dragged the whole lot back upstairs. She stacked a wall of LaCroix next to her bed. Tissues, melatonin, multivitamins, Asshole's supply of power bars, phone charger, iPad.

Then she tore everything off the bed (all except that one particular thing, no, she kept that safe, of course she did, safe and warm) and she dug in the linen closet until she found her old sheet set from college, the soft ones made from some kind of bamboo fiber, or so the saleswoman had said, her first real splurge as an adult, but that was another self, another life. Those worn, tan sheets she now tucked into place on the bed, she pulled on crisp new covers, she yanked and smoothed and arranged it all just so. Then she pulled the top sheet down to make a hollow in the center of the bed, a space framed in pillow-bedding just right to crawl inside. Alone but not alone. Not any longer.

Nesting. You might say Viv was nesting.

———

What now? Well, she would give details, that's what Viv would do. She would flash and splash and show off her wares. That's just the kind of storyteller she is, and who are we to tell it different?

So. It was oval. The size of two cupped palms brought flush together. Smooth surface, the color of a penny moon held up against a black night sky. The outside bone hard. The inside, who can say? You could rap a fingernail on that surface and hear it go *rat-a-tat-tat*.

You wouldn't dare, though. She'd eviscerate you, Viv would.

———

How long she stayed there, brooding, is anybody's guess. She never left her room for more than a quick dash to the bathroom (and honestly, there's a lot you can do with an old pickle jar). Outside, the world carried on: bills and magazines overflowed the mailbox, Amazon packages rose on her porch like a child's tower of blocks, the Prius disappeared under a thick layer of yellow birch pollen.

Just give her time. That's what we thought. She'll recalibrate, she'll come around, she'll reemerge. We did but she didn't, she didn't, she didn't.

She took an extended leave from work. She binge-watched Netflix. But mostly she lay on her side, ankles linked below her butt, knees flush to her chest, arms wrapped protectively around the whole package.

———

On her nightstand, the phone rang incessantly. From the look on her face, you'd have thought hearing that ring was soothing. And honestly, who can say it wasn't? Isn't that its own small seduction, that last gasp of the powerless: the exquisite power of refusal?

We got through to her once. Just once. Oh? You doubt we could get this level of story detail from one conversation? Well, you don't know Viv and you don't know us. It's her job to need and it's our job to know.

Truth is, we caught her off guard. We're not too proud to admit that. Two-oh-something in the morning, it was, and some feeling made us sit up straight, made us creep through the flower beds and edge closer to the window, made us hit *Call*. We watched her press *Talk*, press *Speaker*, her eyes still full shut. We watched her lips move, heard her words in our ears against the hard night air.

She laid it all out for us then. We listened. We soaked it in.

And then—what? Did she stop, did she look up and out, did a glint of eye show through the crack of her half-pulled curtains, a flash of screen in midcall from her dark outdoors?

Ask the silence. Make it tell you what it knows.

———

The curtains are drawn hard against us these days. But we see flashes of movement sometimes, blurring through grime and glass and gauze. Who can say what she's becoming in there, on the other side of the dark? Maybe she's fetal, maybe she's pacing, maybe she's gathering her strength. Maybe she is growing ready to be more than a living shrine to her pain.

Or maybe we're all she has left.

Who can say where the mind goes, when the body can't follow?

MY HEAD
IS A CHESTNUT,
AND OTHER TALES
FROM THE CRYPT

So I've been seeing this new guy, Dr. M___, and he's got a specialty in something called phrenology. Which, if you'd asked me a hot minute ago, I'd have said was some kind of pseudoscience, but this guy has an actual degree in the stuff? Go figure!

I know, I know what you're thinking. I *know*. I mean, what is this, the Middle Ages? Wait, when even were the Middle Ages? I should probably look that up. Whatever. At any rate, I'm with Siri and the rest of humanity on the verdict: This doctor guy's gotta be a quack, amirite?

Well. Here's where things get interesting. (Jk, it's not interesting yet. But we'll get there; trust me.)

———

The first time I saw my own skull, it was kind of love at first sight. Is that weird to say? I mean, my thought literally was: Omg! I'm kind of adorable!

I'd done my CT scan early that morning, and now there I was showing up to my specialist appointment to get the results. I mean, supposedly I knew already what was going on: aka, nothing. I'd found the small bony growth on my left temple a few months before. My primary care doctor wasn't too worried. She said she saw this kind of thing on occasion and told me to just watch it for a bit before giving it too much worry. If it shows signs of rapid growth or change, any pain or tenderness, etc., let's talk again. If not, if it's just hanging out on your skull, not hurting or bothering any old thing, then what's the problem, right? Well, I don't know about that. But whatever: she's the doctor, she calls the shots. I just do what I'm told.

On my way out, though, the receptionist was like, Hey. (She knew what I'd come in for, obviously; see also: receptionist. Okay, plus we'd been chatting a bit during my wait. She knew I was stressing, and I guess she figured out the doctor's stance by my face.) So she's like, No luck? And I shrugged, like, Eh.

So then. Then, get this! She slips me a card. I know

this guy, she says. Well, I don't know him *per se*. Not well, anyway. But he's kind of a—here she made literal air quotes, I kid you not—"Big Deal" in some circles.

And that was my first introduction to phrenology and, more importantly, to Dr. M___.

———

So here's a little 101 for the slow learners, or anyone who snoozed through their pseudoneuroscience lectures back in the day. Phrenology was kicked off at the end of the 1700s by this Austrian dude named Franz Joseph Gall. (The gall of him! I know . . . I crack myself up sometimes.) *Dr.* Gall, I guess, since he was a physician. Or was he?

The idea was that you could tell someone's personality by checking out the shape of their head. Character came from the brain, went the reasoning, with different parts of that organ responsible for different traits. So far so good, amirite? Actually fairly cutting edge, for the time. But Gall took it a step further: When the part of the brain dealing with some trait was more strongly represented or was exercised more, he said, it got bigger. Then it would push up on the skull from the inside, creating . . . a bump! Traits that weren't prominent in a particular brain would shrink down, causing a crater. (Kind of like snakes and ladders but 3D, and inside your head. Also no dice. Whatever, forget board games.)

Okay, so you have all those cool cranial bumps and grooves, and you know each one means something. But means *what*? If you could figure out what parts of the brain-slash-skull connected to what parts of human character . . . hey presto! You'd be both a superscientist and *the* most fun to hang with at parties.

Congratulations! You are now a phrenologist.

And so Gall, and those who came after him, got all up and busy doing experiments to connect those brain-to-skull dots. They had images and models of the human head mapped out into eensy sections, each section marked off and tagged to some aspect of human nature: hope, happiness, strictness, belief, anger, and so on.

Look it up, if you want to know more. Those phrenology charts are all over the internet.

Only—they're not all legit, are they?

———

Just think of your head as a chestnut, Dr. M___ said when I walked into his office. Those were his very first words to me, with a sweeping wave of his hand as he indicated his monitor screen, which he'd swung around to face me as I came through the door. He likes to make a grand entrance, Dr. M___ does, even when he's not the one entering.

And there I was, on his screen, my head in a box. Not gonna lie: I couldn't look away. How often do we get to see inside our own heads? The bone lines were soft and distinctly feminine. Delicate jaw. Dark oval craters for the eyes. Nose cavity dabbed right into the middle. All in all, a fine-looking specimen. Good bones, you might say. I felt my shoulders straightening with new self-respect.

Dr. M___ seemed to get that I needed a moment. I guess he'd been around the block a lap or two. He gave me that time, just sat there with his hands steepled under his chin, letting me get acquainted with the inside of my head. Finally he cleared his throat and waved at the empty chair facing his desk. Please, he said. Shall we get started?

I sat. A chestnut, huh? I murmured.

A chestnut, he agreed.

Sometimes you just know you're on the cresting edge of something life-changing.

———

There are others, you know? he said. Others like you.

Like me?

He waved a hand. A little group I run. Tuesdays at eight. I'll give you the info before you leave. But that's not what we're here to talk about today, is it?

Between you and me, I was just that moment trying to figure out why I *was* there at all.

Dr. M___ pulled out an enigmatic smile, a smile like a bloodred door that you know you probably shouldn't open and yet—

He stood. He pinched the creases in his pressed black pants so they stood out like razors. Then he walked around his desk and came to stand behind my chair.

First things first, he said.

At this point I registered—how'd I missed this before?—the giant mirror behind his desk: a gaudy monstrosity with an elaborately carved gold frame. The kind of thing you'd see in the Louvre, like its own actual work of art. Like anything it reflected would be elevated just by association.

From where he stood behind me, he lifted his hands, flared them out on either side of my head. Not touching anything. Not yet. Just holding there, fingers spread wide, a small tremor rippling from palm to fingertip.

May I? His voice the barest whisper of suggestion.

In the ornate mirror, our eyes met for one gothic,

Anne Rice moment. Then I laughed and flicked my hair off my shoulder by way of a nod and he said, Here, relax now. It's all very scientific, I'll tell you just what I'm doing as I go along.

———

His fingers on my scalp.

How can I describe it? Even now, even after everything. I can still feel them. That very first touch. Never anything less than professional—his voice a murmur as he marked out the terrain of my scalp, pointing out a feature here, a caution there. Combativeness valley and benevolence peak and oh! Look over here in mirth!

I didn't retain a thing. I lost myself in the searing intensity of the moment. I lost myself.

I think maybe I knew even then what was coming: the pull, the power, the cost.

I knew it and I couldn't look away.

———

They formed and then tested their theories in all kinds of ways, Gall and those who came after him: palpating, probing, pressuring. So many skulls, so little time! They found patterns, apparently. I don't even know; science is not my field, nor is history. But it was quite a thing in its day. Like getting your palm read or your star chart interpreted—only this had the shiny stamp of scientific endorsement. For a while, anyway. Queen Victoria and Karl Marx were two of the voices in that chorus, so who are we to judge? It was a time. And those Victorians, they were *all* about this hot new craze: Hey, it was like medicine, soothsaying, and a parlor trick, all rolled into one. Plus, you dig just a little and *poof*! There's your standard-era racism and genderism baked right into the doctrine . . . What's not to love?

So phrenology gathered momentum big-time, starting in the early nineteenth century, first in Europe and then in the US, shifting and growing all the while.

Until . . . it was eventually discredited.

I know! Now we're circling back around toward sanity. (Or are we? Stick with me, baby, I'll show you a thing or two.)

———

He showed me to the Device next—that's what he called it, the Device. Picture this: a cross between a dentist's chair and one of those old-fashioned sit-under hair dryers like in a vintage beauty salon, only with, like, an upside-down glass bowl set on top. Uh.

Why all the belts? I said. Half jokingly, but also kind of like, Wtf?

Oh, that. He waved a hand. Just a precautionary measure. We won't even use them today. Now, if you'll have a seat right here? I think you'll understand better if you experience it for yourself.

So he settled me in, and the chair dipped right back to a neat forty-five-degree angle, ready for business. The mechanism whirred and my head was tucked right under the bowl. The belts kicked in then, latching automatically (arms, waist, legs: *snick*!) and I was like, Huh?

But Dr. M___ was busy at his desktop and I mean, I made the choice to be here, after all. And he's the doctor. So who am I to make a fuss?

My scalp went warm, then ever so slightly tingly.

The chair was tilted to face the mirror so I could join in this semisurreal moment right along with myself. Through the clear glass of the head-bowl I could see a nest of wires humming to life. Each wire had a tiny probe wiggling at the top. I watched my own eyes widen, and then my gaze met Dr. M___'s in the mirror. He shook his head ever so slightly.

It's all right, he said. This is the easy part.

How does he do that with his voice, make it so like a caress, so like a blade?

They had their course well charted, those little probe-wire suckers. They rested oh so lightly on my head—maybe a dozen of them, spread out pretty evenly—then they started to burrow, unsettlingly yet kind of tenderly, through my hair to my scalp. (It helped to think of them as friendly little snakes, or did that make it worse? I'm not sure.) As each landed, I felt the lightest pinprick touch, but that was it. That's the only way I could tell when each probe connected.

I felt kind of badass, tbh. Like a reverse Medusa.

The mirror filmed over into a screen and there it was again, the projection of my skull that I had seen on Dr. M___'s monitor. There was a second—did I imagine this?—when the lower half of the display was still mirrored glass and I could see my body, strapped into the Device, but the top of the frame showed the scan, the image of my bones.

My skeleton head tacked on to my living body.

Then the moment passed and the display was all

graphics and labeled charts and diagrams. Here is your skull. Here are your personality zones. At this point, Dr. M___ went on in some detail about my traits and hot spots and how my skull structure was exactly what he'd been looking for. Balance between the sections, off-the-scale measurements, boundless promise. The word *groundbreaking* may have featured. I'm not entirely sure; I suppose I should have paid more attention, should have asked more questions. It's a personal goal of mine, honestly.

But what I do remember is this: the bony growth on my left temple—the bump that started the whole shebang—this he came back to more than once, stroked it lovingly on the screen with his laser pointer.

This is good, he said. So very, very good. Compliance, benevolence, goodwill. Absolutely unbounded. All this potential, just awaiting release.

You and I, wait and see. Together, we're going to make history.

———

On Tuesday, I went to group for the first time. Dr. M___ warned me beforehand. He was like, Eh, these people, you know. Not all of them are gonna be your crowd. But humor me, he said. Just like that: Humor me. I mean, what was I gonna do. Turn him down cold? So I was like, Sure, you betcha. It could be worse, right? I could be going to my spin class.

It was held in this old community center, the kind of room where you might put out stale sandwiches for the extras in a zombie movie or something. Hardcore basics. Less than that, even. Whatever. I wasn't there for the vibe. About a dozen people were milling around the snack table, chatting and nibbling. On the far side of the room, chairs were set in a circle like some kind of AA / group therapy / kumbaya campfire party.

There was a second there, not gonna lie, where I was like, Wt actual f have I gotten myself into?

But yanno, I was already *there*, and by that point Dr. M___ saw me and he was busy talking to someone but he waved me in, so in I went: slow shuffle, play it cool, you know the drill. I hit that snack table like I meant it. Surprise! No stale sandwiches, but legit bougie foodstuff like seedy crackers and veggies in speckled oil and that cheese that's covered all over with a white crust that's supposed to be edible but I just don't trust it. And Jell-O shots! Okay, probably not *shots*, but tiny plastic cups of colorful Jell-O.

Just as I was thinking I should actually eat something, and what would let me walk away with my self-respect

intact, who did I see across the table but Ms. Receptionist! Of all people! I was like, Janna, what? You? (Et
tu, Janna, right? Nah, I'm joshing ya. That didn't come
till later.) She just looked up from straightening Jell-O
cups and gave me the ol' chin jut. Was she glad to see
me there? I couldn't quite tell.

Dr. M___ came over then, grabbed my hand in one
of his, and kind of rubbed it with the other in this little
pat-a-cake moment. People were turning to look at us.
I don't know if they didn't get a lot of newcomers, or
if the doctor was acting different than normal. I didn't
care enough to dig.

Did you get your prescription? he asked, lowering
his voice so just I could hear.

I came straight from work. It's ready, though. First
thing tomorrow.

He nodded, released my hand, and turned his gaze
back to the room. And I swear, all I wanted was to get
that sun shining on me again. I'd have swallowed the
entire pharmacy for one more second in his glow. He
glanced back at me over his shoulder. Make sure you get
the Jell-O, then. He winked.

Oh. Oh!

He was still watching. I got the Jell-O. I got two.

By the time I downed those, somehow everyone

was sitting. Did I just lose a minute? Suddenly everything was a little loose around the edges, a little wiggly. I blinked to refocus. The faces were all looking at me. Dr. M___ waved an arm. Join us? He patted the chair next to him. The only empty chair. For me! How cute is that?

Not gonna lie, things get a bit hazy after that. I've got flashes of circle time: sharing hour, getting-to-know-you hour. And it was all, After I had my fourth concussion . . . and, Ever since I got my cranial plate inserted I've been feeling . . . and, The hemicraniectomy really messed with my head, dude.

At this point I leaned to my left—away from Dr. M___, who had his active-listening face on—and whispered to the guy next to me, What even is this place?

The guy looked at me funny. I guess he would. But then, I was looking at him funny by this point, because I saw it: He had a lump on his head, just like mine. Or, I guess not like mine, because where my lump was small and basically invisible under my hair, his was pointy and right on his forehead, jutting out like a mushroom from soil. He saw me see it and narrowed his eyes, then sighed like maybe he was used to getting that reaction. But I felt bad even through my haze, so I grabbed his hand and lifted it to my left temple. I rubbed his fingers across my own little bony bit. I could feel the tension leave his grip, could almost hear him relaxing into our shared connection.

His hand dropped and he leaned in close, as we tried our best not to disrupt the general vibe. We call it Head Cases, he said. Unofficially, I mean. Dr. M___ runs it. You know that. He's treated a lot of us, but there's others here, too. Word gets around. You heard 'em—surgeries and concussions and growths, all that shit. Support group, I guess? Some people vent. Some listen. We eat Jell-O. We go home.

I swung my gaze to the room. Something new was happening. The sharing had stopped. People were pushing up from their chairs, smearing the rigid circle borders to fold in here and there along the edges. Janna was sitting with arms crossed and head bowed while a short round woman stood facing her, reaching both hands almost reverently to run them around and along the base of Janna's skull.

And . . . phrenology? I asked.

My new friend grinned. Yeah. That too.

———

Things did start to unravel, eventually, for Gall and the phrenology flotilla that followed him. (Whoa! Say that five times fast!) Part of it was all the bickering among the various factions who couldn't see eye to eye on how many character hot spots ye olde skulls had—twenty-seven? Forty? X+Y=Z? Plus, if you're gonna judge human behavior by the way the brain pushes up onto and impacts the bones of the skull, I mean . . . isn't the next logical step to go down *through* that skull, right into the actual brain itself? Yeah, nineteenth-century science thought so too. Bone saws at the ready!

So phrenology fell out of favor in the mid-1800s. And you'd think that would be the end of it, wouldn't you? But this stubborn pseudoscience hung on, kept on circling the drain of oblivion but never quite snaking down to actually disappear. There was an active British Phrenological Society clear into the 1960s! And when you think about all the ways brain science has advanced since then, and how the brain really *is* parceled out into very specific zones and regions, each of which does accomplish a specific task in cognition and acquisition and even personality—

Well. Who's to say what is really *pseudo*, when you come right down to it?

———

Or so Dr. M____ would have us all believe.

Me? I was still reserving judgment.

Or maybe I was just too stoned to care much one way or the other.

————

In this way, time went by. Weeks. Months. Tuesday night as community, as worship, as god. Late summer became fall became first snow. We hunched closer in our chairs. The Jell-O turned frosty winter shades. Hot new hues, same great taste.

We learned more about Dr. M____'s vision. A great vision. The greatest!

We turn our backs too quickly on the past, he said. Lectured, really. He lectured. As for the rest of us? We blinked, we listened, we refocused. We listened some more. On he goes: But the past is always out there waiting, isn't it? In our rush to embrace modernity, sometimes we overlook the roots, the true foundation of our society. The bedrock which brought us forth.

So what you're saying is—

Someone new was speaking, cutting right through Dr. M____'s stream of words. This was unusual. Mostly we didn't talk, outside of our circle intros and personal updates. Mostly we listened and tried to look like interested sponges and pondered the texture of Jell-O. Or was that just me? But this was—oh hey, it was my forehead-growth pal from my first time in group. We hadn't talked again since; somehow he always seemed to be on the far side of the circle from wherever the doctor sat me. A few times he started in my direction during the mingle, but someone always seemed to step in front of him, or Janna or the doctor would tug me away somewhere and the moment would pass. Now, though, he was all intent, all laser purpose, chasing the A for his Q.

What you're saying is you're actually taking it all seriously? This phrenology stuff? Like, you're planning another comeback for it or something?

Dr. M___ considered. Well, Hugo, he said. You're here, aren't you? Why *are* you here?

Hugo snorted. He looked at me, like he was considering. Taking something in. Eyebrows up, shoulders set.

Some people, said Dr. M___, prefer a hypothetical view of life. They like to keep their words suspended in amber, framed under glass, hung on display where they can be trotted out like a set piece and shown off or debated or whatever else might suit their carnal inclination at a given time. But we—

He stood now, he strode now, he (how did he do this?) was a mile tall now, we had to crane our necks to look up at him look up into his face look at—

We do not just speak. We act.

Hugo fell away. We all fell away.

———

There was a break. Another break? Another night. A blizzardy, blustery night. But group must go on! People were hitting the Jell-O table harder than usual. Dr. M___ was giving me the eye. I went for thirds.

We sat. Circle time was over, and Dr. M___ took the floor and talked. Lord, how he talked! I tried to listen, god to Boy Scouts I tried! Tonight's was extra impassioned too, all, We have come to a critical crossroads . . . and, This next step will forge our scientific future . . . and, Who can I count on for next week? I need a volunteer, just one person to help me make history.

I looked up then. Okay, I'd been checking out my phone just a bit. I mean, can you blame me? But the moment I did, he was all up in my psychic space. I shoved the phone back into my pants pocket. I took in the moment and it wasn't lost on me, the six other hands flapping clear around the circle and him ignoring them all and looking only at me. (Suck it, Janna!) The whole room was silent.

His lips moved without sound. He held my gaze. He was mouthing a word: *Chestnut.*

I couldn't help myself. I cracked up.

Whatever. He wants me this bad? I'll be his precious guinea pig.

———

Have you heard the story of Mary Rafferty? His voice was quiet over my shoulder as I stood on the front steps of the community center, looking out. The snow was still coming down. I tried to make out my white Corolla but it was playing peekaboo with the drifts. I shook my head and the world spun in slow circles.

The year was 1874, he said. Roberts Bartholow. What a doctor, what a man! This Mary, a patient of his, she had a nasty head ulcer. Came out through her skull, ate that bone clear away so her brain was on display. Right there in the open, can you imagine it?

I refocused. I tried my best to imagine it.

Well, it was an opportunity, wasn't it? Her brain was *right there.*

Someone trudged past us down the steps. Janna. She

turned to padlock the big door at the entrance behind her, then plowed down through the driving snow and disappeared.

I knew I should be contributing to this conversation. There was something important about this story, if I could focus enough to capture it. Something he wanted me to know. So, I said inadequately, what did he do? About the brain.

Electrodes were so rudimentary in those days, weren't they? And still, *and still*. What an effect! Just one probe inserted directly onto—*into*—the brain matter itself! Done. And what did they find? Imagine it. Just picture how that external brain stimulation correlated directly to movements, to the subject's *involuntary* movements, to personality expressions quite outside her intended control. Can you see it, hmm? One zap and—*bam*: She smiles. She laughs! Even as she screams in pain, even as tears bathe her cheeks, Mary Rafferty never stops laughing. That—ah, my dear—that is *science*. And now! He reached a hand to twist a strand of my hair and tuck it behind my ear. How much more could one do now, with science and medicine so advanced, so very far advanced?

Just one well-placed electrode. Imagine what could be done!

What about, I struggled to get the words out through

gluey lips. What about the lady. The patient. Mary Rafferty. What happened to her?

Dr. M___ looked at me, frowning. Well. She died, didn't she. A few days later. Pity. So much more could have been explored. He puffed out a sigh. Come on then, you're in no shape. I'll drive you home.

———

Was it next week already? It must have been, because I was in Dr. M___'s office. Guinea pig reporting, as promised! The mirror behind the desk was a magic mirror, it was a mirror that was also a door and that door opened and I was led through and it seemed like a good time to close my eyes and rest. Just for a minute. I'll be fine if I can just scrub that crust off the cheese. Then I'll be good to go again, I know it.

Meanwhile? It's showtime.

———

Hello, you.

Where am I? But my words sounded only in my head.

He leaned forward with infinite slowness. And—how

could I have missed this? In a sudden bolt of clarity, I saw. This exquisite snail's pace he'd been moving at was not caution, was not care, now, was it? No. It was relish, it was anticipation.

It was foreplay.

The long straight razor moved closer to my head and my vision blurred trying to follow it. The smoothest steel kiss on my skin, then a rush of cold air at the side of my scalp.

Naked? I've never been naked before this moment. Keep going, I wanted to say. I concentrated on trying to get my lips to form words.

All the history books, he murmured. A curl of hair slid off the blade and I wasn't sure if I wanted to laugh or scream. Forget Bartholow and Rafferty. We will be the ones to rewrite the narrative. Carve it from our own sweat and blood. Me. And you.

But. (Words at last! My mouth was so, so dry. Where's a Jell-O shot when you need it?) Why a chestnut?

He smiled then. Was there a pattern to the smiling moments? There was something there, if I could just think clearly enough to connect the dots.

Don't you know? Well. You have to crack a chestnut open, don't you? To get to the good stuff inside.

He turned his head to look at someone just out of

my line of sight. You have the electrodes ready? She should be ready in fifteen. Maybe a little more solution, just to be safe.

———

Will it change me?

I wasn't sure if I'd spoken aloud or if these were just more words pinballing inside my brain, cushioned on bouncing beds of Jell-O. But from the lift of his eyebrow, I saw that he'd heard.

This operation, I mean. You said it's safe, it's routine, but I know it's also . . . experimental. Right?

I wouldn't say *change* you. Not exactly. He seemed to be weighing his words carefully. I suppose I would say—free you. Just think of your head, that magnificent brain. He tapped it again, my bony nub. This here? I call it the compliance zone. Even in its wild state, see how it pushes up, how rich a vein lies below, buried, untapped. That's what first drew me. All that potential! To give. To yield. To *do*. Exactly what I've been looking for.

He leaned in closer. He set his silky hands on either side of my head, then gently twisted my neck so I could look right into his eyes. Just think of all you have inside there, locked away behind that wall of bone. What if that

wall wasn't there? What if I just opened things up . . .
right . . . *here.*

He traced a finger slowly, reverently. X to mark the
spot.

What could you do then, hmmm? What could
you *be?*

————

A movement to my left. Even floating on the fringes of
sensation as I was, even so, I could sense her, I could
see her. I hated her. I hated her for being part of this
moment. My moment.

Hush, Janna said. Here, take a sip of this. This is
good work you're doing. You'll see. You'll be right as rain
again in no time at all.

I wanted to ask what this meant for my current
rain. Wasn't it right enough? But my lips were gummy
worms and the cup at my mouth was tipping up, so it
was choke or swallow. And oh, doesn't the sweet poison
go down slickest?

Good girl, she whispered. You good thing. There
you go. Just you keep smiling, just you keep laughing.
There you have it.

Over here, Janna. I'd never heard Dr. M___ sound

so clinical. Pass me the cranial drill, won't you? And the saw, while you're there.

———

A lurch. My eyes popped open.

I didn't seem able to move, but as I scoped out my small, darkish space, I could tell I was in a vehicle. A moving vehicle. Thick straps held me tight in place. I faced backward, but the labored breathing and tuneless hum from behind my head told me the driver was Dr. M___.

I could not believe my clarity of mind. What was it he'd been messing with inside my brain? Compliance zone? Well, I felt . . . great. Amazing, in fact! As though all the rules, all the constraints and control of the last months—of my whole life, honestly—had peeled from me like gum off a shoe.

Reborn, that's the word. I felt reborn.

I bucked hard against the belts holding me. My left arm sprang free. The belt snicked back into the armrest.

Wait. I know this chair.

The Device is . . . portable?

At an odd pulse in my temple I probed, very gingerly. The left side of my head was wrapped in a thick bandage. My bony growth? Gone. There was no pain to the touch, just a vague, squishy sensation that curdled my stomach. I dropped my fingers fast. I yanked at my right arm, pulled against the bands gripping my waist and the one leg I could reach. Nothing gave. I guess one arm was all I was getting free.

Even that arm was not entirely out. A tube fed from it into a small portable IV, though I couldn't tell if it was in use or not.

And yet.

How amazing was life? The tuneless hum at the front: one of my favorite songs. His voice, too. What vibrato! And these driving twists and turns, we seemed to be on some kind of mountain road. A bit of a skid at each turn—snow and ice, very likely. Oh, and there's a burst of speeeeed!—how very like a roller coaster, a roller coaster on ice! Glorious.

I craned my neck back, arched my spine to see what else I could make out. No glass dome on the Device today, what fantastic luck! My gaze followed the curve of the vehicle's roof—not especially high up, so not a van. Some kind of long, tallish car, I supposed. Sized to fit an operating chair tilted nearly horizontal, with space for straps and bindings and IV to boot. Impressive! Great thinking, Doctor. Still farther back and the roof

crossed into the front, over the driver's seat. No divider
between the two parts of the vehicle. And there was the
top of the windshield. By now I was arched as far back
as I could, just enough to see full into the mirror.

There: a reflection. Two wide, startled eyes. Surprise!

Goddamn it! I'd never heard Dr. M___ swear, but the
force in this one made up for it. The car swerved briefly
as he lost control for a moment. Goddamn that Janna,
I told her to give enough . . . Hey, you okay back there?
He slid on his winning smile, in all its best bloodred
polish. I felt curiously unaffected. There was so much
inside me already, so much unfettered self-contentment.
What more could he offer?

I'll be right back there to give you a hand, he said.
Something to drink. Just hold on while I find a spot to
pull over.

The inside of my chest felt so, so full. I'd never ex-
perienced this level of joy. This was something special,
something more. This required an offering. It required
action. Some blockage to remove, maybe. But what?

Once again I felt there was something, just at the
edges of my mind. I couldn't quite put my finger on it
(so to speak, har har!), but oh, give me another hour or
two and I knew I could recapture it. Yet an hour was
one thing I clearly did not have.

And so. If your whole swelling self is a wave cresting, a swarm massing, a bomb ready to fling burst blow go—

Well. What would *you* do?

———

It was nearly as quick to think as to do: A tug of my free arm to release the IV cord. A swipe to grip the stand. One quick dip down for momentum and then a hard fast swing—using every bit of my strength—back behind me.

The thing of a moment. The thing of a lifetime.

Compliance? Oh, yes. I am indeed unfettered. Just see how unfettered I can be.

Then I let go.

I opened my hand and let my projectile fly.

———

It took a while for the car to stop spinning, stop turning head over head over head over head. I had a fair time to admire the truly incredible manufacturing that went into these belts. I was yanked side to side, sure, but not a beat beyond that.

On the bright side, I'm safe as a button!

On the, well, I suppose you might call it the *less bright* side, I'm still strapped into my chair.

The screaming from up front has stopped. The moans too. There's just a whimper from time to time, but I expect that won't last much longer.

It's awfully cold in here. I can't see anything through the windows. It seems to be nighttime, and I have a strong suspicion that we've landed in a snowbank. Oh, and the vehicle seems to be upside down? I don't have a lot of immediate options, but I do have my phone with me.

I know, right? How amazing is life! There it was, right in the left pocket of my cargo pants, where I always put it. It was powered off but that was an easy solve. I don't have actual cell reception, which is too bad.

So that's why I decided to do this recording. I don't have a huge social media presence, but lately the app has been all, Record Offline and Post When Your Connection Is Restored! Cutting-edge technology meets cut-edge technology . . . omg I crack myself up sometimes.

Welp, I've done what I can do. As soon as my signal comes back my story'll upload itself right on up to the cloud, into the rain, and back down it'll go into all those little devices all over the world. Someone will be out there. Someone will get my message. Come to the rescue, all this way out into the wherever-we-are. How long does it take to trace a signal?

My battery's at 19%. There's still time.

Meanwhile? Things couldn't be better.

SONATA IN GOD MINOR

She only took the blues class because he wanted her to.

"You never play anymore," he said, speed-packing his travel bag a half hour before the Uber was due, as usual. "You're going all dry and wasted. Gotta get back that spark, eh? Have some fun while I'm gone."

Well, fuck me, Kia thought. She rolled over and flipped the sheets dramatically. "Fun is you coming back to bed. You've got, what? Twelve minutes? We can work with that."

"Don't you remember back in the day, those music intensives you'd take? Whole days, weeks you'd lose yourself in your strings. You'd fly out to Saint Louis or

Cincinnati, come back with some new guitar each time and you'd just have this *glow* . . ." Bryce leaned over to kiss the tip of her nose. "Damn sexy, woman."

Kia narrowed her eyes at him. "Glow?"

"Look," he said. "I found this blues workshop you'll love. It'll be good for you. Get you back to actually playing some of those guitars you keep locked up in that room, on your trophy wall. Do it for me? I prepaid, even. All you gotta do is show up. You can thank me later."

Since the night they'd met in the mosh pit all those years ago, they'd been inseparable, he'd been all she needed, he'd filled all the gaps. Why should it be any different now?

Kia grabbed the nearest pillow and flung it at his back. "I'll show you a fucking glow!" But it *was* different, wasn't it? Already her mind was probing, flexing. Tasting possibility. Already on her skin: a shiver.

"You're welcome." His easy laugh scratched down the dark column of her spine. Damn him for knowing her so well, damn him to hell.

———

That was the worst of it: she *had* started wasting. Bryce was good for her, so good, just what she needed. He appreciated music, but distantly, mutedly. He was the calm to her tempest. The muffle to her roar. What Bryce didn't know, what Bryce could never know, was how much it had cost her to turn her back on metal all those years ago. How much her fingers still ached for the exquisite pain of the strings. Even now, she just had to hear the right hard-driving beat, those notes torn and tortured just so—and she was gone.

But blues? Blues were sweet, blues were soft. Blues were safe. And so much time had passed.

What if she did take this blues class? Soft, melodic blues, that was the actual name, Advanced Soft Melodic Blues Guitar, like that would really bring all the serious musicians flocking in? Well.

Honestly. Why the fuck not?

———

So now here she was, at 9:00 a.m. sharp, wedged into an old-fashioned wooden chair-desk, right at the front of the class under the nose of the blackboard.

Just kidding! What the actual fuck? She chose the online session, obviously. Never pass up a gamble, her godfather used to say, but always keep one hand on the escape hatch. Then again, look where he'd ended up hanging.

In any case, Kia was just glad she didn't have to change out of her nightwear before she wandered into the music room to log on for class. She did briefly consider getting dressed, but why bother? Raw silk: fabric of the gods.

The workshop started right on time. When the morning session kicked in before the zero was off the nine, Kia nearly blacked out on principle. Nothing this punctual could possibly be worth it. She kept her camera off a few more minutes, driving that point home to herself and taking the time to study her fellow blues-mates. There were three women—a gray-haired Asian woman in her twilight years, a white thirties house-wife type with actual curlers in her hair (wtf?), and a prepubescent-looking prodigy with long bangs and longer nails (and how did that even work on a guitar?)—along with eleven entirely interchangeable men.

The instructor, though. Here was something else, here was something interesting. What it might come to, she couldn't say. Only, for now, just this: an itch.

On the surface he was nothing special. For one thing, he was disturbingly young-looking. He had blue eyes and mouse-brown hair and the uneven jaw stub-ble of a kid still figuring out razors. From the looks on the fourteen other faces in her zoom window, Kia wasn't the only one developing a class theory: What the fuck's this man-child got to teach us anyhow? He looked like a strong wind could knock him into bed. Not her bed, obviously. But still.

"Hiya, gang!" he said, validating her darkest expectations. "I'm Stuart Truman, but you can call me True Blue Stu. Or, you know, just Stu is fine." He chirp-laughed, and it was so painfully dorky that it was nearly adorable. Nearly, but also not. With a sigh of resignation, Kia patted down her bedroom hair and turned on her camera.

"Ah!" TB Stu pulled a pick from behind his ear—Kia died a little more inside—and tapped it against something out of the camera's view, like maybe a water glass. "Our final member appears. Shall we kick it off with introductions then, class?"

"Good morning, Mr. Truman, I'm—" Curlers woman jumped right in. Kia gave her mental points for assertiveness.

"*Stu*, please." He interrupted gently but firmly. "I insist."

The woman looked briefly rattled, then gave a short nod. "All right. Stu. I'm Sandra Lassi, and I've been playing guitar since . . ."

Kia zoned out. She much preferred to make her own assumptions about her classmates' pasts. That was always more interesting than real life, and (bonus!) kept her occupied during the long, tedious instructional parts of class. *Advanced*? Please. What Kia would take from this workshop, she wasn't ready to predict, but guitar instruction would not be it.

———

The morning sessioned on.

After introductions there was some lecturing, some listening to prerecorded blues pieces. There were small breakout rooms to work on group assignments. Kia let herself enjoy the music distantly, safely. Whatever Bryce might think—bless his nonmusical heart—*losing herself* was not an option here. So she kept her background safely on blur and angled her guitar off-screen. She kept her playing tame and controlled. She kept it safe.

And yet.

Hour by hour, she found the man-child's soft, melodic blues growing on her. Growing in a way that scratched at the inside of her jaw and prickled up toward the base of her skull. Growing like the shadow of a long room hung with ghosts. Growing like temptation, like a pulse, like a drug.

She held back, she held on.

She held.

By early afternoon, Kia's nerves were sharpened to a raw edge. More than once she thought of bailing altogether. But her godfather hadn't raised a quitter, and by damn she was worth six of him.

Still, this? Fuck this. Kia snapped off her camera. She set her Strat back on its stand. It wasn't escape time, not yet. But her internal warning lights were shading orange. Stay alert, you goddamn weakling.

Just a few more hours to go. She was no longer sure if she was trying to prove something to Bryce, to herself, or maybe to that long-gone figure from her past—but she'd see this workshop through. She'd see it through and then she'd lock the beat away again for a good long time. Maybe forever.

Yes, she could do this. She could keep control. Exposure therapy, wasn't that a thing? The cure is the cure. The fear of fear is the fear. Or something.

Kia's phone buzzed. Bryce? No. It was an unknown number.

?

Kia ignored it. Then glanced at the Zoom screen. Oh, hell no. TB Stu was frowning down at something

on his desk—his phone, apparently—and completely
ignoring the musical prowess of Miss Prodigy, who was
fingerpicking her heart out on the latest assignment.

Where did you go?

She saw now that she had a string of personal mes-
sages in the classroom chat. Kia sighed. She pushed her
phone to the far edge of the desk, then clicked into the
chat window.

Sorry! Tech problems, no
more vid ☺ Am here tho

On-screen, something rippled across his face, but
the reply in the chat was brief:

ok

Was that tension she could see building below the
surface? But Stu just brought his hands together and
broke out a Sunday-morning smile. "All right, gang!
Shayla, great riffs, great stuff. Now I want to move on
to something a little different."

Kia felt a cold stone settle in her belly. There is a

moment, her godfather used to say as he placed his bony fingertips on the blades of her shoulders, as he pushed her down. There is always that one spot on any slope that is the point of no return, a moment when the balance tips and what is begun can no longer be undone. If you know yourself, child? You will know that moment.

In the speaker box on her screen, Stu grinned and his cheeks actually dimpled. "I wasn't sure I was ready to bring this piece out for today's class, but what are you gonna do when the gods call your name?"

Kia shut her eyes. She could still see the dark glint on the old moon face above her, eclipsing the world. You will not be able to stop it, he would say. But you will know it.

And she did.

———

So it began. Stu pulled up his guitar, Stu flipped his pick, Stu began to play. He began to play and it was almost visible, how the notes poured out liquid and went for her throat. Even still holding, even still fighting—I am not the stone, the stone is not me—Kia felt her whole body shudder.

"You get me?" Stu paused midstrum, leaned right

up close to his camera. "When the gods call? When you hear that call, you bring your dues and you pay up."

Without music, he was just a diaper in dress-up clothes. But with it? Kia braced herself on the desk with both hands as the shiver rippled up her forearms. It wasn't that she just heard the music, or that she felt it, not even that she was swept up in it or lost in it. It just . . . was there.

It was there and it was air and it was light and sound and—

Kia could feel her vision tunneling. Stu's blue eyes were somehow enormous, filling her monitor and tangling with the notes. The scratching in her head was back—no longer growing but grown, it was in her now, it was inside her bones—filling her body, filling up her brain. Kia stabbed frantically at the keyboard. Where was the goddamn fucking escape hatch? Around her the music swelled and grew and—

———

Kia blinked.

She came back to herself in a dark room, facing a blank screen. The only light came from the pale bracket moon in the black sky outside. The day? The rest of the whole fucking day?

Okay. So. Not the greatest start to her controlled reentry.

But look: Here she was, intact. Alone. Safe.

Kia took stock. She sat in her desk chair, back straight and body angled slightly forward. She held her Strat upright in front of her—one hand on the neck, her bare knees wide to hold the upper bout—everything she'd ever need, you might say, all wedged in the tripod of her body. She fingered the keyboard, brought the screen back to bright. A page of sheet music was up and open. She considered the notes.

Well, she was here, wasn't she? It was just her and the dark. Why the fuck not?

She hooked the step stool with her toes, dragged it over and propped her bare foot on its quilted top. She set the guitar over her knees. In the shadowed room, its glossy flank looked black and the black looked good enough to lick.

There was a pick in her hand. 1.14, all right. Thicker than she preferred, but she was in the zone now, no time for adjustments. She swung her arm and pulled on the air in a grand sweep, reveling in the big-feel drama: the hum, the build, that trapdoor moment before the hangman's pull and the drop.

And then . . . she played. Slow at first, tentative,

exploring the strings like the body of a lover she hadn't touched in years. Hey, you. Hey there. How does this feel? You like that? Right over here. Mmmm, yeah.

It had been so fucking long. Oh sure, she'd played a bit here and there. Even in the session earlier, she'd held her pick and strummed the notes and shown up for the beat. But not like this. Never like this. Not since—

No. Kia prided herself on her self-awareness, but there is only so far you can sink and still live with your reflection in the morning. And this—oh, godfuck, *this*— was what she'd been missing. And she hadn't known. Hadn't let herself know. How could she? This was weakness, this was yielding, this was abandonment to the forces outside her control.

Spark? And then some.

Her phone buzzed.

No way in hell she was leaving this moment. She swatted the phone and it slid off the desk to buzz against the carpet, lower but still insistent. Kia kicked it under the desk, reset her foot on the step stool, went back to shredding.

———

A minute or an hour later, she was pulled from her musical trance.

The doorbell?

It couldn't be Bryce, obviously—he'd use his key. In any case, he wasn't back till tomorrow and it was barely 8:00 p.m. Though you wouldn't know it for the dark outside. There was literally no one else who'd be showing up on her doorstep.

Or . . . was that still true? Something itched like phantom claw marks in her brain. Kia scanned the desk for her phone, remembered, didn't feel it worth the hunt. Propping the Strat back on its stand, she moved to the window. She twitched the curtain and looked down toward the front stoop, but the night kept its secrets.

The bell rang again. Something hot and hard and hungry pushed in her gut. Kia shoved back. Cursing, she threw on her robe and belted it tight, marched down the staircase. She flicked on the porch light and flung the door open all in one motion.

"Hey." There he stood, breath steaming in a frosty cloud around his head, ungloved hands rubbing together.

"Stu," she said, her voice flat. "In the flesh. What are you doing here?"

He ducked his head and she saw he had a case strapped on his back. A guitar case. Obviously.

Kia shut her eyes and steadied herself on the doorframe.

"Can I come inside?" In the half-frozen yellow light he looked so, so young.

"That's not a good idea. You should go."

"I can't. I, uh. I walked here?"

"I'm sorry." She took a step back and pulled the door shut, but it stuck. She looked down. His booted foot was jammed into the space.

"Look," he said, and—there. Desperation? Need? It twanged inside her. No. It didn't. "Just let me warm up. I don't want anything, I swear. I just thought we could jam a bit. You know, like we said?"

"Said?"

He waved his phone vaguely in her direction, not so she could read any actual words but clear enough that she saw the flash of her own name and a whole string of texts below it. Fuck.

"Look," Kia said. "I don't know what I said earlier and I honestly don't want to know."

A crease formed between his brows, taking another five years off his ridiculous baby face.

Kia clenched her fists. She puffed air out through

her teeth. "You can't stay. You just can't. Trust me on this, it's in . . . everyone's best interest."

"Five minutes? I'll warm up quick, I swear. Then I'll Uber home."

She let the words hang in the frosty air, let them turn to iceflakes and float away on the night. Waited to see what he'd do with them. His blue eyes never blinked. His gaze never left her own. What *had* she texted him?

Finally Kia spun on her heel. "Don't take off your boots. Wait right here in the hall. I gotta get something." She stopped at the bottom step and frowned back at him. "Uber."

———

The phone took her forever to find. What was under this desk, a passage to Narnia or something? But she finally got it—without cracking her head open, bonus— and quickly scrolled through their text exchange. It was worse than she'd expected, better than she'd feared. She deleted the chat, powered off her desktop, and as she turned—

"You in here?" TB Stu was poking his head around the door, because of course he was. The fucking glory of human nature.

Kia could have said a lot of things. Specifically, she could have gone off about intent and will and self-control and how in the end, nothing—goddamn-fucking nothing—mattered, and why? Because what would be would just goddamnfucking be. And wasn't that just the fucking way of things. But what would be the point? Instead, she flicked on the desk lamp with-out a word. She pulled the door open and moved to the side, letting Stu into the room, then shut the door behind him.

He had the grace to look sheepish. "I waited down there for ages. I was starting to get worried." He waved his phone, frowned. "It keeps restarting. Uber, I mean. Is it your signal out here? It said nineteen minutes, then it said twenty-five, now it's at like thirty-eight?"

Kia kept her hands on her hips, kept her eyes on his. He ducked his head, and if he was trying for nonthreat-ening, he was owning the part. He had lost his jacket and in his crimson shirt he looked like a plucked chicken. She shook her head. "I'll try mine," she said, waving her phone at the room. "Couch. Minifridge. There's some IPAs in there. Help yourself."

He leaned his guitar case against the couch and pulled a beer from the fridge. Then he turned to take in the long narrow space, the well-filled walls. She waited.

Sure enough: "Wow," he breathed. He walked slowly down the room, twisting his head side to side. "This is—this place—how many guitars you got hanging up here? I'm not sure I've ever seen this many types—and all this coloring. What a range. Wow!"

Kia showed him her teeth. "Eleven. They're all unique. Individuals."

"I can see that." He grinned and leaned close to study one of the nameplates. "Each with its own name, too? I've heard of people doing that. Never seen 'em posted up on the wall." He laughed but Kia didn't join in.

"Yeah. It helps me remember."

At the far end of the room, Stu stopped in front of the huge statement poster that filled the wall. "Dude," he breathed. "Xavier X. Monticello? *School of X*? Are you kidding me? How did you *get* this?" He leaned in closer. "Is it *signed*?"

Kia let him have his moment.

He leaned in, moved back, paced from one side of the poster to the other, taking in every detail, stopping every few seconds to shake his head. "What a guy—what a guitarist. You saw him play?"

Kia's lips twisted. "You could say that."

"That man was a legend. Probably the greatest metal guitarist who ever lived." Stu took three steps back, bumping up against the couch, then popped the lid on his beer can and took a long swig, all without taking his eyes off the poster. The figure in shadowy silhouette; the long, sinewy limbs balanced on the tall stool; head bent low over the guitar; bony features obscured in the art but carved indelibly in Kia's mind.

"Wait." Stu pointed at the label below the guitar that hung next to it. "X? No name needed? *Oh my god*, was this one *his*?" His voice actually trembled and he stepped forward. "Can I touch it?"

"No," Kia snapped. It was suddenly all too much. "No, you can't touch . . . it. Now, can we move on to something else?"

Stu turned and stared at her. "You knew him."

Well. Why not? "He was my godfather, actually. He raised me. From when I was eight until—" She barked a short laugh. "Yeah. You could say I knew him. You could say he taught me everything I know."

Stu dropped onto the couch, took another long pull of beer. She could feel the force of his gaze settling on her. "That explains it, then." When she frowned, he wiggled his fingers in a pantomime of fingerpicking. "You were holding back. In class. Don't bother denying it—I could tell. It still came through, though. It came through big-time. You've just—there's something about you. The way you play. Why d'you think I'm here? I didn't fully get it before, but now . . ."

Kia shrugged but he went on.

"You must miss him. I mean. I know he's been gone awhile, but still—if you were close . . ." He shook his head, maybe processing the look on her face. "I don't mean to keep bringing up painful memories. Forget I said anything. God, I'm such a dumbass."

"No, you're fine," said Kia. She rubbed her clammy palms against the sides of her robe. "Will you—give me just a sec?"

She turned and left the room, and heard Stu call over her shoulder. "I'll try Uber again, see if it's any better."

Kia staggered into the bathroom and turned the cold tap on full blast. She filled her cupped hands, brought the whole mess up and flung it at her face, did that again and again until the freezing water drenched her hairline and pooled around her neck. It coursed in icy runnels down the open neck of her top and dripped the length of her body. Taking ragged breaths, she leaned over the sink and let the water fall where it would. She shook her head hard. Then she padded back into the music room, the tension in her chest building with every step.

"You get it, don't you," she said, facing him, breathing hard. "You get what music is, what music does? The power. The pull. What it can do if you let it."

"*Let* it?" He grimaced. "Is that the way it works in your world?"

Kia pushed her wet hair back from her face. "Do you ever feel like sometimes the whole world is . . . spiraling out of your control? And then other times . . ." She wiggled her fingers, flexed, squeezed them into fists. "Sometimes it comes back, comes *to* you. That thing you don't want, that thing you're trying so hard to resist. It comes and it comes, no matter how hard you push it away." She laughed shortly. "The point of no fucking return."

Stu set down his beer and stood up. "Shouldn't you listen, then? If you can't fight the hunger, why not . . . embrace it?" He took a step in her direction.

Kia took a step back. "That's the thing about hunger, though, isn't it? Once you let it in, once you let it take hold—how do you know if you'll ever be able to turn it off again?"

Stu closed the space between them in three strides. He put his hands on her shoulders. He leaned in.

Kia jerked back. "That's not what I—" She shook her head, moved toward the door. "I'm sorry about the Uber. I couldn't get a signal to lock either. Damn weather. You can stay on the couch if you want; it should be better tomorrow."

Stu stayed motionless in place, hands still raised, half attack, half defense.

"There's bedding in the cupboard there," Kia said. "I'll see you tomorrow." She turned and left, shutting the door behind her.

———

Outside the music room she stood still, breathing slowly in and out. Then she reached down and—very quietly— turned the lock.

Back in the bedroom, Kia took off her damp robe and nightclothes and flung herself on top of the duvet, where she tossed and turned like a ship in storm.

She needed Bryce, needed his grounding, his silent safety. But her gaze kept drifting to the doorway, her mind kept winding down the dark, silent hall. The music room was fully stocked with pillows and blankets and all the shit you'd need if you were crashing unin- vited at somebody's house. Stu would be fine in there for the night. Still, the pit in her belly churned and churned.

Distantly, the locked door gave a low, insistent rattle. The silent night rang with unbearable music.

———

Kia sat up in bed. She crept down the hall to the music room door and set her palms to the slick, painted surface. She turned her head and pressed her cheek against the cool wood.

She could hear a breath hitch on the other side.

"Kia?" His voice was the barest whisper. Then: "I know you're there."

She sucked in her own breath, held it until she couldn't any longer. Then she turned her back against the door, slid down the smooth length of it and dropped silently to the floor, knees pitched up like a tent and jammed against her bare chest. Kia ran flat hands along her calves, up and down, slid them around to cup the backs of her thighs, tugged hard to crush herself into the circle of her own body.

"Kia?" His voice was a little farther away now.

She opened her lips.

She let go.

"Play for me," she whispered. She sprang to her knees, spun around, and flung her body at the door. It was no use fighting. It had never been any use. Or . . . maybe this *was* fighting, maybe this was fighting the only way she knew how, the frenzied throes of a cornered beast. Maybe the real danger had never come from without but from within. Kia threw back her head and arched out her chest and let the word—let the power—carve itself bloody from her core in one long primal scream: "*Play!*"

Spent, she dropped back to a crouch. Her forehead met the door with a low thump while in her mind and in the air, in the hall around her and under the door and all through the locked music room, the word turned and spun and rang, echoing, echoing: play play play play play play *playyyyyyyyyy.*

There was no discernible response from inside the room, but seconds later it started: the low pull of flesh on string, the tugging of torn guts into music, the bleed of notes into a sonata of pain and power and transformation.

Kia kept her palms flat on the door, her head hung down, panting, panting.

When dawn broke the hall was quiet.

Kia stood. She unlocked the door and stepped inside.

She opened the curtains, quickly turning away from her reflection in the window and its damning, telltale glow. The music room waited, silent, breathless. Stu's guitar lay discarded on the floor. She set it back in its case, then latched the case shut and stood it by the door. She walked the length of the room and back, pausing to press her fingers lightly on each hanging body in turn. Respect. It was the least she could do. In memoriam.

Only then did she turn to the couch, to the long, motionless figure draped in blankets. To her surprise, her face was wet. She scrubbed at her eyes with the backs of her hands. There was space on her wall. There was room for one more. And this nameplate would only need three letters.

"Oh, Stu," she whispered.

She pulled away the blankets to reveal the new guitar. With gentle hands she hefted it up, ran a finger down its crimson flank, its mouse-brown strings. The tuning keys in the head were so very blue.

IN THE SHADOW
OF THE ABYSS

You don't take a photograph. You make it.
—Ansel Adams

It was as though she'd never left the pool: never did, never could, never would.

They'd found the island on yet another humid day on the high seas, summer, or what passed for summer in this part of the world, where every day had the same consistency: thick and soupy with a fug that leached all the water from Karenna's pores and sent it cascading to the base of her spine. Even the headwind off the bow barely lifted the tips of her bangs. Then, between one eyeblink and the next, there it was—a bright-green thumb jutting from the pale seasky they'd been drifting through for what seemed like forever.

They dropped anchor a ways out from the beach. The yacht couldn't get any closer, Adam said, which made sense to Karenna, or would have, if she'd cared enough to give it more than a passing thought. Instead, she busied herself getting ready for landfall, stuffing essentials into her overnight bag and cushioning them around her photography equipment: lenses, flash, tripod. She slung the underwater camera around her neck. By that point, the inflatable was ready and Adam was bellowing for her, so she zipped the bag shut and made her way above deck. Anything else she needed badly enough she could make a trip back for.

As usual, he'd done twice the work in half the time and was waiting for her to say so.

"Wow," she managed. "Twice the work in half the time. You're a wonder."

"Come on," he said, indulgently now. The kiss he dropped on her head seared straight down her middle.

Slightly breathless, she followed him down into the dinghy. He made such a picture there, her husband: bronzed skin set hard against the dead blue water, straight dark hair in the low breeze rising and falling, rising and falling. She thought if she could capture this likeness of him, if she could hold him somehow to the here and now, it would answer some question inside her that she couldn't quite shape into words. She pulled out the camera and had it halfway to her face before he noticed, grunted, and gave her his back.

Karenna sighed. She swung her lens toward the island instead, did it in a smooth enough arc that it might have been what she'd intended all along. Adam saw and raised a finger to point the same way: redirection as peace offering, the Adam Muller Story.

"You see?" His voice popped with excitement now, words cracking a bit at their ends. Karenna could almost hear the teenager he had once been. "Look at this beauty. Paradise! Didn't I tell you?"

"You did," she murmured. And then, because it was true and she couldn't help saying so, "It's gorgeous. It's perfect."

Karenna shifted position and lifted the viewfinder right up to her eye. She knew it was old-fashioned, but there was something special about the act of bringing the camera to her face. It blocked out the rest of the world, isolated the shot in a way that just wasn't replicated by looking at the display screen. An image was a moment, was a lifetime, was a world, and if she could see it—truly see it—then she could capture it, and maybe keep it forever. That was why she sometimes liked to watch movies with the sound off. Imposing your own reality onto the world around you, the Karenna Muller Story.

Somewhere in the near distance, Adam was mid-lecture. "They used to be volcanic, all these islands. Like underwater mushrooms, hundreds of them strung along the continental crust. A hundred million years ago, this was all one big underwater reef. Think of that!" He paused. Karenna zoomed in. *Click.* Back out again. "Amazing, isn't it?"

Through her lens, the island was dark and brooding and dramatic, like it belonged on the cover of a pulpy thriller. Like the hero you know is bad news but can't tear yourself away from. Was there something familiar about it? She shifted, raised herself to a half crouch, examined the angle critically. *Click.*

"Isn't it?"

"Oh!" Whenever Karenna was startled, she felt a sharp run of prickles down the back of her neck. She pulled herself back to the moment. "Yes, so amazing. I didn't know any of that."

He was still scowling at her camera so she powered it off, let it swing down between her breasts. "Tell me more," she said brightly. "You read up on the area before we set out?"

"Nah," he said, and she could hear the tension drain from his tone. It was so easy to keep things good, to *be* good. So easy. She just had to stay focused. "Nah. Just stuff I know from keeping my ears open. It's a big world out there."

The putt-putt motor carried them easily across the jostling waves, each one sending up a fine-mist spray that was more tease than balm to her sweaty skin, while high above, the merciless sun beat and beat. Karenna leaned back on her elbows, let her eyes drift shut behind her sunglasses. She would have stripped to nothing if she thought she could get away with it. Instead, she let one arm drag behind the boat, fingers dipping below the water's surface. She could hardly tell where the air ended and the ocean began.

Then, a jolt. The scuff of rubber on sand. They'd arrived.

Before the boat was completely grounded, Adam hoisted his pack onto his shoulders and hopped over the side. "Come on, look alive," he called back.

Karenna frowned at her feet, wishing for the water shoes she'd left on the yacht. She leaned over to fumble with the straps just as Adam gave the dinghy a sharp tug onto dry sand. Karenna lurched sideways. She flung her arm out to brace her fall, felt the thick side rope skid and burn down her inner forearm. But she managed to catch herself, so: a win.

Behind her, Adam gave a grunt of frustration. "Seriously? Keep an eye out, Kady. I can't do everything."

Karenna blinked, and somehow Adam was ten or twenty feet up the beach, taking long strides away from the shore. Had she just zoned out? She grabbed her sandals in one hand and her duffel in the other. "Coming," she whispered. But for whose benefit? She rubbed the back of her neck absently.

She'd expected the island to feel bigger up close. But even from here—especially from here—it was preposterously small, a stage designer's tropical dream set. Still, there was an air to the place. Karenna felt a dark churn of excitement in her belly. Something was happening, something was coming, something was *here*.

With the dinghy secure, she put on her sandals and plunged after Adam into the underbrush. In her head she was suddenly a carefree kid again, a seafaring explorer mapping out a new land, casting the old away forever. She glanced over her shoulder, pulled up her camera and snapped a shot of the beach—dinghy in the foreground, yacht moored in the rear distance. *Leaving the Past Behind*, she titled the image in her mind.

What if it could be that easy? What if, just like that, all the unpleasantness, all the scenes, all that murky *badness* could just be in the past? Left behind forever. Maybe that's what this place was: a beginning. The chance for something completely new. She just had to be better. She turned and ran to catch up. Adam hadn't paused, probably hadn't even noticed her absence. She smiled, let out her breath.

The scrub went from the shore's hardy, salt-scoured stuff to a finer, deeper verdigris the farther inland they pushed, sandy silt giving way slowly to dark, loamy soil. Within minutes, the foliage was so thick you could forget you were on an island at all. The ocean was a distant memory, a dream of another life.

"We're definitely going to camp here for the night," Adam said. "We've had enough of that yacht for a lifetime, haven't we, babe?"

"For a lifetime," Karenna agreed, although she loved the cabin and its small, safe embrace. Not to mention all the stuff that hadn't made it into her overnight bag. But she could rough it for a night or two.

"I have a good feeling about this place," Adam went on. "We'll find a flat spot with some tree cover, pitch our tent. You can cook up some of that awful campfire mush you love. Living the dream!"

His tone was teasing and light. Karenna felt herself lulled by the moment. "It really is magical here. Even the air smells different. Not the kind of place where anything bad could ever—" She bit the words off abruptly. Maybe he hadn't heard. She cut her gaze sideways. A muscle in his jaw tensed, but that was it. She let her breath out slowly. *Just be better.* She could do this. She could.

A moment later, they pushed through the last of the tree cover and into a giant clearing, like a bite taken out of the island's heart. In the center, framed on all sides by ungainly scrub trees, was a wide, crystal-blue pool.

Dropping her duffel, Karenna took slow steps toward the shore. The water called to her in a voice she couldn't quite hear. She could not look away.

"Earth to Kady?" Adam's voice seemed so far off.

There was something about this water, this pool, the way it thrust itself at the turquoise sky and gave back as good as it got. The edges so blue it made her bones ache. She raised her camera, framed the shot. She frowned, lifted her eye from the viewfinder. What *was* that? Seen only through the lens: a long, dark shadow in the pool's center.

"Hey." His hands were on her shoulders now, his face in her face, eyes narrow and assessing. "What's going on? Where are you?"

Karenna blinked. Water lapped around her ankles. "Oh, goddamn it," she said, snapping back into the moment. "These were my good sandals."

———

There is a dream she always comes back to, every time her eyes drift shut even for a moment. A dream that feels so real, too real, that pushes insistently at the walls of her mind, that wants to be let in.

She will not allow it.

———

They made camp on the long edge of the clearing, near a bush studded with big red and purple flowers, each one the size of a fist. Adam pitched the pup tent while Karenna stoked a lackluster fire and reconstituted their dinner. Through it all she kept her back to the siren water, tried not to catch it even in the corner of her eye. Still it insinuated itself into her thoughts, dug at her mind like a finger in a wound. It was exhausting.

Finally she stood. The pool wasn't going anywhere. Well, neither was she. Karenna spun and met it head-on, met it and faced it and then—why the hell not?—marched down to meet it. Behind her she heard Adam drop his bowl and scramble up. Ready for another intervention, no doubt. She flapped a hand to show him she had it this time, she was in control.

It was just water. Just an ordinary body of water. Karenna let her breath out slowly. Holding your ground, that was the thing. You could spend your whole life cowering, turning away from things, but what did that accomplish in the end? She breathed in the heady, freshwater scent, ran her gaze along the surface, a clear, unbroken blue from end to end. No shadow. Not even a hint of one.

Adam came from behind and twined his arms around her shoulders, locking her against his chest. Her hands itched for her camera, but it was back in the tent. She pictured herself at the viewfinder, studying the pool, scanning for dark things unseen by the naked eye.

Light through the lens, trick of the leaves. That was all.

"Where do you go?" Adam murmured in her ear. "You've been doing that more lately. Disappearing into your head. Going places I can't follow."

Karenna shrugged. There was something about that shadow. Even in her memory: it undid her.

"You'd never leave me, Kady-bear, would you? Not for good, not for a minute even. You'd never go, would you?"

She could feel his heart pounding a tattoo on the column of her spine, could feel the rhythm of her breathing ease to match his. She unclenched her fists and shut her eyes and tipped her head back onto his shoulder.

"Of course I wouldn't leave you," she murmured. "Not ever. Not even for a minute."

What an everlasting picture they made. Against the black of her lids, she set up the shot: It would be taken from the side, the two lovers in three-quarter frame, one thin and slight against the other's steadying bulk. Behind them, the hungry dark. Before them, the water, bleeding out the dying day. At the last moment, the slight figure swings her head around, looks straight into the lens.

There is no expression on her face at all.

Click.

The thing was, she knew Adam was right. She *had* been losing herself more lately, dropping moments like so many clicks between shutters. But the pool, the pool. It held something, it said something, if only she could manage to hear it. *I'm listening*, she told it. And then, *I'm coming.*

"Hey, check it out!" Adam had released her and

wandered back into the trees, and now she turned to see him holding a pale-green fruit half the size of his head. His wide-spread hands didn't even span it fully.

"A pomelo, really?" she said. "Here?"

"I've never seen one anywhere near this big." He jogged closer, tossing the fruit from hand to hand, looking like a boy with a plan. He cranked his throwing arm back and she readied herself for the catch, but at the last moment he twisted position and pitched the fruit in a hard fastball, straight at her middle. Oh, she knew him so well. She should have seen that coming. The direct hit socked her back several steps. Her hands came instinctively to her middle, holding the hard fruit in place against herself even as she struggled for breath. She needed to be better, be better. Why hadn't she seen it coming?

"Brilliant save!" Adam was all easy laughter now, the tension lines gone from his face, his shoulders jogging up and down. "Way to stop a drive-by fruiting." He ran to her and swept her up in a giant bear hug and she let herself sink into him. It was almost—she thought, as her insides loosened enough to pull in a gasp of air, as sensation crept slowly back into her extremities—almost worth it.

———

There is a dream she always comes back to: a shadowy image, rippling and indistinct, seen as though looking up at it from underwater, an image she might almost be able to reach if only she were strong enough, if only she could break through the surface into the air and grab it with both hands.

There is something here. Something important. Something she can almost remember, if only she would let herself.

As always, she sinks too deep and the moment is gone.

———

Later, they sat side by side on her old throw blanket at the water's edge and watched the sun go down on the trees. It was spectacular: a charnel of crimson and bloody gold filling the skybowl above so that every bit of world around them glowed red.

"It's like being in a gullet," Karenna whispered.

"In the belly of the whale," said Adam. "Isn't that the story? Three days and three nights or something? Fucking catechism."

Karenna frowned at the pool, which lapped and licked at her toes. She leaned forward. "Look out there. You see a dark spot right in the center?"

Adam laughed. He flopped onto his back and tucked his arms above his head. "Oh my god, listen to you. This whole clearing is one big shadow and you're creeping on one in particular?"

Karenna knew she should let it go. But his eyes weren't even open. "I saw it earlier. Then it was gone. But now it's back, in the exact same spot as before. And look, there's nothing above it to even cast a shadow. No trees, nothing. I'm just saying, it's weird."

"Kade. Listen to yourself. We've talked about this already. We're not here for mysteries, we're here to chillax. Summer sun, tropical island, the whole drill. You know that."

She did know that, just as she knew that no good would come from pushing him. But there was something about that shadow. She couldn't leave it alone. "Isn't there some big underwater wall off one of these islands? It's a thing. I read about it in this diving magazine. You can swim down and follow it and it just goes and goes. Way into the deep. It drops off the edge into an abyss or something." In spite of the heat, she shivered.

"So go," he said carelessly, but she heard the whetstone strike just below the surface. "You know so much from your magazine reading, you wanna go mystery diving? Go on then, go find out. Go now."

Karenna winced. Why was she like this? Always pushing. Always too much. The same old Karenna, no matter how she tried to be new. On the blanket next to her Adam's hand opened and closed, his eyes dark and shuttered now, his breath speeding up. Karenna ran her fingers along the blanket's knobby, woven surface. She needed a distraction. She needed— There.

"Look who it is," she said, grabbing the pomelo and hefting it up. It was surprisingly heavy, like a very small human head.

Adam looked up and gave an ice-pick grin. "Ah. The offender in the flesh. I'd say it's time to teach this bad boy a lesson, wouldn't you?" He sat up and grabbed the pomelo from her, tossing it hand over hand.

"How do you even eat one of these?" Karenna tucked trembling hands under her legs.

"Don't be ridiculous. It's like a grapefruit, only bigger. And sweeter. You know how to eat a grapefruit, don't you? You just go at it, peel and devour."

"How do you know all this stuff?" The words came almost on their own by now. She was starting to breathe easier. It was good to know what to expect from a person, from life. They weren't out of the red zone, though. Not quite yet.

Adam speared her with his gaze, bringing the

pomelo very slowly to him. Then he lunged at the rind, one wide bite savaging the top clean off. All the while his eyes pinned hers, daring her to look away. She didn't even try. He held her a few moments longer, then turned to assess the torn fruit in his hands. Karenna felt herself sliding down a wall, allowed herself one long breath of release, of escape. The shameful thrill of making safety one more time. She did not think it should feel this exhilarating, the gazelle leap to freedom, however temporary.

Well. She might never be better but goddamn it, she was still here.

The bitten-off fruit top was jagged in his upturned palm. He brought it toward her. There was still glass in his gaze—it was melting, but not fast enough. She could see this next, petty violence play out, and it would be so easy just to absorb, it would be nothing, less than nothing. Instead, she turned at the last moment, let her head fall back to bare the long stretch of her throat, opened her mouth wide. She met the fruit, thrusting toward it, and she took it in, took it pulp and peel alike, bit down and chewed and felt the sweet and the bitter churn together until there was no telling what was what, bit hard and let the juice run down her chin and into the aching hollow of her body. She swallowed it all.

"Here," she whispered. "Now how about I show you something *I'm* good at?"

And he was hers again.

Adam worked his fingers at the big body of the fruit he still held until the thick rind came off in his hand. Tossing that aside, he pulled off a segment and brought it gently to her mouth. She closed her lips around it, feeling the sweet-tart juice running through his fingers and filling her mouth. Above them the sky darkened further, like violence seen from the inside out, like a wall descending. But wasn't it a metaphor, she thought, the whole belly of the whale thing? An illustration of purgatory or some such?

Or maybe it was none of that, maybe it was just humanity, pure and simple. Just life.

They shared the rest of the fruit and Adam licked up the juice where it had doused her chin and her neck and slid down the front of her dress. She laughed and loosened the drawstring so the top gaped a bit more, nipped the last segment from his fingers and nudged his leg with a bare toe.

"Lemme see all that," Adam said, and he turned to face her, sat up and swung a leg over to straddle her low across her hips. He tugged suggestively at her sundress and she laughed.

"This?" She flipped the dress's hem up and down. "This is what you want to see?"

By way of answer he grabbed his T-shirt and pulled it over his head in one smooth motion, and she couldn't help it—her breath caught in her throat. He was so god-damn beautiful, this husband of hers, all windswept hair and full lips and busy, moving hands. Her dress came off next and he leaned down over her belly.

"Oh," he whispered. "Just look at your poor skin, look at the work of that nasty old pomelo." He hooked a finger under her chin and traced a hard line straight down, cutting clean through her center, then looping around to trace the wide bruised circle of her middle. She propped up on her elbows to watch him as he studied the spot in evident fascination: the flat smooth of her abdomen with its jagged darkening center. It was just going purple now, but she knew well the rainbow of colors waiting up ahead. She tried to remember what she'd done with her one-piece bathing suit, then smiled. What did that matter here? They were the only ones around.

Adam lowered his head to her belly, dropping a string of kisses that circled a hair's width from the hurt. He circled tighter in then, testing with his lips and pushing at her purpling skin with his tongue. Karenna let her head drop back behind her, felt her gaze go unfocused as the pool and the sky and the land flipped places, turning head over head. It hurt and it hurt and it hurt and somehow she wanted more. She sank deep and hard into the moment as if it could last forever.

———

There is a dream, but it isn't a dream. She knows that for sure now. A dream wouldn't have this hard insistence, this brutal knife's edge that won't stop carving its way into the fascia of her mind. Why won't it let her go, let her drift, let her rest?

It won't. But if not a dream, then what? What do you call a moment that traps you in its dark embrace, clings hard and pulls you under, all the while pinching your eyes open and forcing you to look, to see?

The past. You call it the past.

———

For several hours into the night Karenna held herself still, making a sort of game out of keeping her breaths shallow, daring herself not to move a muscle. Adam had the tent set up just as he liked it—a little close, overwarm with the mesh windows all shut—but with time, that came to feel a bit like safety. She lay spooned tight to his front, her head resting on his muscled arm, the hard pillow of his bicep gone soft in sleep. She could almost hear the underwater roar of blood pumping through his veins. It was a curiously soothing sound. Her bruised stomach throbbed under his grip, his hand still flexed hard in sleep. Was it too early to try? Experimentally, she arched her back and edged sideways. She counted silently to five, then eased out the rest of the way.

A minute later she pushed through the tent flap, pausing only to grab the camera before inching the zipper shut behind her. She gulped the night air in one enormous breath, winced, forced in another. As she moved toward the shore, a soft cling on her bare toes. She looked down to see the ground strewn with red and purple petals.

Karenna looked back at the shadowed tent. The thought of that deflowered bush standing stripped bare, unseen in the darkness, made her feel curiously undone. She lifted the camera: black on black, with the peaked canvas roof at dead center somehow looming darker than the rest. *Click.*

Still aiming her lens, she swung to face the pool. She could almost taste the breeze that curled off the water: moonlight and memory and a hint of something floral on the edge of decay. The moon as high and hot as a spotlight. One step forward. Then another. And there—*there*. A thrill went through her, apprehension and tension and a dark, twisting pull that hissed like a hot breath in her ear, whispering, *Come*.

Karenna knew, her rational mind knew there was nothing supernatural about the dark spot in the center of the pool. It was just some underwater formation playing tricks with the light. And yet—on this night, under this sky, in this place—somehow, she didn't give a fig for what was real. She'd come ocean to island, island to clearing, clearing to here, to now, to *this*. And here now *this* hung before her like a gift. She could simply reach out and take it.

If only she were bold enough. If only she dared.

The water licked the backs of her knees, crept up her thighs, slipped inside the elastic of her white cotton underwear. She brought her bent arms up to her face and dipped low just as the ground below her dropped off an edge and she was under.

Under.

First, there was only darkness. The spotlight moon cut the surface, but only so far. Karenna lifted the camera and peered through the lens as her eyes adjusted. Algae, rocks, schools of tiny fish . . . She pulled deeper, probing with her camera from side to side, feeling the breath pushing at her lungs. Searching, always searching. *Where are you?* She needed air.

Back above water, she took in steadying breaths as she paddled in a circle. The pool was not wide and she was nearly at the midway point. She could be back to shore in no time. The treetops overhead kept watch, placid. Karenna kicked onto her back, lifted the camera. *Click.* She sank slowly and water splashed over the lens. *Click.* The moon gazed round and regretful. *Click.* The topside world twisted and warped, a view shaped by the deep, as though seen from a long way away.

She flipped to her front, aimed the lens down, pushed deeper.

Streaky light spears from the surface played peeka-boo with this underwater world, teasing objects in and out of sight, showing, withholding, giving, taking away.

There.

A bend in the underscape, a glimpse of a shadowy crevasse edged in jagged rocks. She'd found it! But she was out of air, again. Frustrated, Karenna kick-shot her way to the surface. She forced herself to take slow breaths, to channel the breathing techniques her yoga instructor had taught her—Kumbhaka Pranayama, breath retention. She was good at it, too, she could breeze past the three-minute

mark with little effort. Okay, not too far past three minutes, and that run-in with the pomelo would keep her
from any new records. But you could swim a long way in
one hundred eighty seconds. You could go deep.

Floating on her back again, Karenna took in the dark
sky, seared and marked by a spray of small white scars.
Did the night mind, she wondered, this perpetual disfig-
urement? This constant show of never-healing wounds?

Finally she was ready. She expelled the last of her air
in a whoosh. Took one large, life-affirming gulp, as deep
as her bruised insides would allow. Then she hefted her
camera and dove.

In seconds—knowing where she was going this
time—she saw the dark shadow looming ahead. She
pushed harder, letting the camera drift on its strap, using
both hands to propel herself.

It was just a black hole at first: a great, gray-black
formation looming in the murky near-distance, half-
seen in the filtered moonlight.

Farther. Deeper.

Then, a flash of clarity. It wasn't a hole, that
shadow. It wasn't an underwater wall or well or any
kind of formation or construction. She took in the
rows of jagged, pointed edges . . . teeth? The gaping
round edge that extended just beyond her vision . . .

a jaw? Larger than life, as the saying went. Suspended in front of her, motionless.

Inviting.

Karenna expelled the tiniest thread of breath, extending her underwater stay. Her lungs felt no pressure at all. Not yet. Moving her hands in small circles to keep herself in place, she considered what lay before her. She thought back to what lay above, sleeping, waiting.

She dove.

She swam deeper as though toward memory, as if into time more than place, swam right at this thing she knew suddenly she must capture, must recapture. She swam at the gullet and toward it and into it. Karenna dove and she dove and she just kept on.

———

And here she is. But has she ever actually left?

———

The day is inordinately hot in this dream that isn't a dream, this memory, this moment she finds her way back to at last. It feels portentous somehow, inevitable.

So: She is here. The day is hot, the kind of slow-burn

swelter that crawls under your skin and chews you from the bones out. They settle early in the backyard by the new in-ground pool and stay there all day, chasing the ghost breeze that occasionally blows up the hill, that skitters around their manicured lawn and lifts the edges of their pointed sun tent and gives its sparse relief. Like so much in her life, Karenna thinks, it's so very little, so very late.

She's been in and out of the pool all day. She keeps thinking the water will cool her down, but every time, it's like dipping into a vat of backwash. Adam, meanwhile, hasn't stirred from under the tent in over an hour. He's reclined with a book, his legs stretched out long and tan from his colorful swim shorts. What are those weird green fruits on the pattern called? Some sort of citrus, like a cross between a grapefruit and a lime. She'd wanted the bikini in that design for herself, but she knew better than to buy a two-piece. Go ahead and tempt fate, why not. She'd told Adam her dilemma and he said why not get the trunks for him instead, so she did, figuring he'd never be caught dead in something that bright. Instead he's worn them every day this summer. She chooses to view this affectionately. And isn't perception ninety percent of reality, when you really get down to it?

Adam frowns at the page. She takes him in: bronzed

skin gleaming, straight dark hair rising and falling in the occasional breeze. Six years together and her husband is still the most beautiful man she's ever seen.

"Hey," she calls from the water. "How are you doing over there? How's the book?"

He doesn't even glance up. The shadowy island on the front cover gives her the creeps, like a goose on her grave. He's been obsessed with the book for days, all big talk of buying a yacht someday and going "island hopping." That's the literal term he used, like the boat might come with seven-league boots and you could just leap from place to place. But to hear Adam tell, it would be paradise: "Can't you picture it, Kady-bear? Summer sun, tropical island, the whole drill. That's the way to chillax, let me tell you."

She's been on her top game today—all her best efforts are lined up on his side table: spiked lemonade, salt-free corn chips, plastic cup of just-picked red and purple peonies—hoping to set him in a good mood. She needs him happy, needs him docile, needs to keep the peace for just a few more days. Just till everything is ready.

She makes her voice light as foam. "You should come in the pool with me for a bit. The water's awful, but it beats the air any day."

He looks up then, looks her dead in the eyes. His chin is set and a muscle tenses in his jaw. Karenna feels her breath hitch as her thoughts kick into high gear. When's the last time he turned a page? What is that glint in his lap . . . *Where is her phone?*

Karenna pulls herself out of the pool and takes a step toward him. The breeze lifts a loose peony and sends it spiraling to the ground. The back of her neck prickles.

He hasn't moved, hasn't taken his eyes off hers. "Hate that I call you Kady, do you? Call me your own names, do you? Controlling. Over*bearing*. That's what you say about me when I'm not listening?"

Her mind races, rat in a maze, chasing pathways in her mind and knowing they all lead to the same dead end.

"Didn't we talk about this kind of thing, *Kady*? Weren't you just telling me you wanted to *be better*? Honestly. It's not that hard." He jumps up so abruptly that the side table and chaise topple behind him. Her phone flies one way and his book goes the other, landing so hard it cracks clear down the spine. Karenna can't tear her gaze from its two broken wings. Red and purple flowers spatter the tiles. He steps forward and she steps back, feels her heels scratch up against the lip of the pool.

"Please," she says.

He tilts his head. Sizes her up. Drops his voice to a dead-still hiss. "You don't get it, do you? I *know*. The list, the plan. The *escape*? I saw it. I know it *all*."

She can still think of something. She can still save the moment. Her gaze snags on his patterned shorts. "Pomelo," she whispers. "The design, the fruit, that's what it's called, that's—" Her nostrils are full of the scent of crushed petals.

"You want to go swimming? You don't need me for that." He is on her and his look is not anger, it is glass, a hard pane of glass in the moment before it shatters. He closes the space and she tenses and he brings his fists up low and hard and fast and they catch her square in her middle. "You want to leave that badly? So *go*."

Her body absorbs the impact. She tips back toward the water in slow motion and her gaze stays fixed on his as she breaks the surface and he never looks away, his expression as she sinks never wavering and where is her breath, did she leave it up there with him, did she leave it back on the pool's edge, because in her lungs there is nothing. She remembers yoga class, she can hold it, she is good at this, but no, she is still sinking and god everything is going blurry and what is all this water, so much water . . . And there, up through the deep, she can just make out the rippling, indistinct image on the surface, its round, regretful face as it studies her and maybe a shrug, maybe a tilt of the head and a turning away and a moving back into the sun and then—

—and then one long shadow, falling over everything.

STORIES I TOLD MY DEAD LOVER

*In order to rise from its own ashes a phoenix
first must burn.*
—Octavia Butler, *Parable of the Talents*

There are stories you run from and stories that kill you
and nothing in between.

I know you can still hear me. You don't know what
comes next, but you want to hear my story.

It's so dark out here. How am I going to tell this
story if I don't have any light?

I've got five matches in a black lacquered box and
nothing else to show for my life. I don't know if it will
be enough. I've got five matches and the world is dark
and here beside me your body is already growing cold.

———

You came to me first in a fog of cigar smoke, in a penned-in corner of the dark, in the char taste of scotch and saliva. You came to me and you scored me and you made me your own. What else could I have done? Even now, even knowing what I know, I think I would have followed you anywhere. But I had school the next day. So I smoothed my red party dress and I grabbed my puffer coat and you were gone. I didn't even know your name. Yet still I tipped my head back to taste the rain and I hop-skipped every puddle home. I was the luckiest girl in the world.

I searched for you, after that. Let my eyes endlessly roam the crowds, kept my ringer on in class, wore holes in my Converse trudging up one street and down the next. I snuck out at night and shadowed the doors of every bar in walking distance: standing with my hands in my pockets and my eyes full of need. It would be a while before I learned that you can't hold smoke by grasping it in your hands. You can't dig the well by wishing. You can only seal up what you've kept inside until it settles and becomes a part of you. You seal it and you hold it. You call it enough.

Until one day, even that is no more.

———

There is something about sitting with the dead. A certain porous listening, a lack of presence that holds a strange presence of its own. A wake, some might call this, when in fact the opposite is true. At any time, in any given place, the opposite of any state is always true. It's called conflict. It's called tension.

It's called life.

———

That's one match down: just one brief flare and then gone.

The second encounter took years to come. Eventually I managed to mostly forget you, in my coming-of-age glowup, working those teen-movie tropes like so many boxes on a checklist. I wouldn't have called it meanwhiling. I wouldn't have said I was holding my breath.

Did I know you were still out there, biding your time? I can't be sure.

That's the thing about hindsight, isn't it? The shroud it winds around the past, so sheer that the contours of our lives edge through, but opaque enough to keep our darkest secrets buried. And us? We look back and call it wisdom, when it's nothing but smoke and swirling grave dust. After all, that's why we have stories.

But late one night at Shauna's basement party there I was, there you were, there we were. Another box ripe for checking: the clarinet, the crowded room, the tangled gaze, the jolt of recognition. Boom.

You? You. Thin, this time, wiry rather than rounded. Heavy scruff on the jawline. A little taller, or maybe the opposite? So it was with Shauna's parties. Still, for me you were enough to vaporize the room, suction up all my self-control, turn my bones fully to liquid. Always, ever, you were enough. Everything else lost meaning.

A dance or two. A drink or six.

I fell into you. I remember nothing else.

Days passed. Weeks. To me, a lifetime. Such is the paradox of youth. Such is our greed, such is our arrogance, to believe we can squander our hours and days in an orgy of forgetful abandon, as if they, as if we, will never die. The fountain of youth flows up but the sand in the hourglass flows down, and time is an occupying force which takes no prisoners and leaves no survivors in its wake. That's the truest lesson there is, and the best of us learn it early and well. For the rest, there is memory.

So. There we were: rumpled sheets and empty takeout cartons and screw what's left of the real world, if it even still exists. You were mine and I was yours and I would have gone anywhere, done anything, to stop time from ever moving forward again.

Run away with me, you said.

And all I could think, all I could say was, *When?* was, *Just say the word!* was, *Yes* and *yes* and *yes.* We will travel the world together and we will be all we need and do you see? I am already gone.

I waited a full day and night for you at the bus station.

When the gut-gray dawn finally brought under-standing I left my duffel on the bench and neatly folded and stacked next to it: my scarf, my softest traveling sweats, my undergarments, my brand-new Converse bought for the trip.

I walked home bare and I swore that park bench was the last piece of me you would ever own.

———

Well. Some believe the germ of every future growth is embedded in its first small seed. Is the life we lead our choice or our inescapable fate? Can a soul be its own architect and jailer and inmate all at once?

So much time has passed, but now in the end it's

just me and you and the empty dark. No one else to call. No one else to need. Not anymore. Just two chairs on an old wooden deck, and off down the hill-side below, the rolling thicket of roads not taken and paths not walked.

Two matches are now burnt down to nubs. How many to go?

Are you counting?

———

I got strong, after that. I swore I would and this, at least, I did. There's never been a more empowered woman. I racked up degrees like trophies, displayed them as such. I met a wonderful man. Love? I can't say for sure. But contentment. Respite.

There was never any question of children. I knew enough to draw that line on my stone-cold hearth.

But life. It went, it moved, it happened.

Why is it that things feel smoothest just before the jagged edges start to bite through? Why that never-ending search for better, never mind if better is that very thing we are tearing apart to escape? I started going out in the evenings. Leaving late. Staying later. Matty worked indiscriminately, and you might say he could have noticed, could have been there, could have cared. You could suggest a hint of shared blame. But I claim no one's demons but my own.

It took a lot of walking, a lot of drinking, a lot of dark descent before I found my poison. And even then, it wasn't found by searching. You came to me—wasn't that ever and always the way? That day at the water's edge. Say I was feeding the seagulls. Say I was taking in the view. Don't say I was gripping the guardrail with white-knuckle hands, drawing force from the steel like a coiled spring aiming up and out.

Then behind me: a low cough. I froze. I didn't have to turn. I knew it was you.

Different, again. Hair longer, darker. Face younger. Body chiseled. Skateboard in hand, even. But that gleam in your blue eyes? That never changed. I loosened my death grip and I turned and I met you, stare for stare.

Something for the pain? you offered.

I jutted out my chin. Shuttered my gaze. I looked a fright, how well I knew it. Yet you could always see me. See through me. You had a way of pushing past that sheen of normalcy to my smoldering core that always lay building, building. Just awaiting your spark.

What is it, in the end, that separates life from death? So little: A whisper. A breath. If we are lucky. But beyond all this, if we can only look back from that final brink and know we lived. And oh, how you and I lived! That day on the bank turned into a leap entirely different from the one I had planned, but leap I did.

I walked away from my old life that afternoon and never looked back. I flung myself in your wake and we leapt into each other and were filled right up. I vanished. I was a snake swallowing my own tail and was swallowed in return. There was nothing we wouldn't try, nothing we wouldn't do. It was heaven. It was hell. It was madness and I let myself sink as low as I could go.

And when the darkness came—and the darkness always comes—I planted my feet and I took the hits as if they were my due. You were always so loving, after. So tender. Even when your attention started to wander, when two became three, became four, became an endless parade, I found comfort in what I thought I could still control. I was strong. I was holding on. Even this, I could overcome. That strength I drew from you, from us, it could be enough. I could be enough.

I should have known from the start that it was always going to end as it began: on the broke-edge of night, all the lost time at my back and the roar of life loud enough in my ears to block out the big questions:

Why am I here? What am I doing with my life? Who am I?

The thing is: It's not enough to ask those questions. You've also got to listen to the answers.

———

That's three matches down. We're getting closer to the end now. I know you can't hear me, not anymore. So why do I go on? Why tell my story? Maybe it's for the night birds as they circle low, stalking their prey. Maybe it's for the wind, as it takes what it wants from the branches overhead, neither asking permission nor giving apology. Maybe it's for the rocks as they sit and stare and never say a word.

Or maybe it's for none of those.

Maybe it's for anyone who might hear it and who might yet escape.

———

What is that old line about saving the best for last? Who-ever coined that phrase never knew you. Life may be an endless row of peaks to climb, but never forget that every slope has two directions. When your eyes are fixed on your feet, it can be hard to tell the horizon from the cliff's edge.

I saw so clearly the twisted paths that had brought me this far. I understood, now, what toxic was. But secretly, I also believed in change. I believed in hope. What I didn't understand was that the deepest shadows were not outside me, but within: that never-ending want, that shattering hunger that recognizes the dark and yet makes the same choice, over and over again.

And so. Here you were, one last time. This new you. This familiar stranger.

As ever, you took my breath away. You were calm and sedate and just the right amount older than me. A bit of hair loss around the temples, but I quickly learned not to bring that up. Your deep-brown eyes saw into my soul. When you smiled at me that first time, the storm clouds parted and for a moment I was that little girl again, that puddle jumper, that sunshine believer. Oh, how I wanted to believe! I heard your words as you promised me the world. This time around, I swore, everything would be different. Once again, you made me yours; I swallowed you and your silken words alike. Once again, I lost myself.

It didn't take long.

Your strictures, when they first came, how small they were. How reasonable. Always answer the phone.

Never leave the house after sunset. Decline all unap-
proved invitations. The list of appropriate activities was
long enough, after all. Infinite choice within my preset
boundaries. I told myself I deserved this. Look at my
own choices and where they'd led! You unquestionably
had my best interests in mind.

Structure. Boundaries. Limitations.

It could work.

Is it age that wears down that shroud of hindsight?
The moths of time chewing holes in our rosy backward
view, letting more of the darkness show through?

If only.

I was desperate, don't you see? I needed a solution to
this problem, the problem of *me*. And there you were, as
ever with your magnetism, ready to solve all my problems—before they arose, even. And this new you, this
new man so loved by everyone, this time around you
were better than ever. Strong to my weak; smooth to
my rough; level ground to my ever-shifting sands. You
coated me from head to toe. Every wound, every hole
carved out of me over the years, you flowed in to fill.

Then again—that was always you, wasn't it? Doing
the carving with one hand, patching the gaps with the
other.

I fit so well on your shelf. The shiniest, prettiest

object in your collection. Mask in place, plastic smile at the ready. Bendable. Biddable. Just exactly so.

Until what? Where did the first crack come from, where did it begin? Somewhere between *I never could have imagined* and *We all saw that coming*.

That's where the kindling lies. Waiting only for a spark.

———

Such a small flame, the head of a match. Such a small kiss, to hold in its lips the power of utter destruction. Four matches are gone, four lives lived, and with them the course of my own past. What do I have left to show for it all?

My story here is told and the sky above me is full dark and in my box one match still remains. One match. One deck. One life.

A choice? You really think so?

It's already gone.

———

One day, when they ask me why I burned it all down, what will I say? What answer could I possibly give but this: that I was here and he was here and sometimes a life, a world, it grows on you like a cancer; sometimes it grows and it fills and it feeds and you bleed and you change. You make space and you grow and you become and finally, you are. You *are*.

Then, one day you're digging in your closet, and you hit that plywood wall you threw up decades ago because the mind is not always a weight-bearing surface. You hit that wall and today it strikes you different, today it strikes you slant: not a surface, maybe, but a ledge. And you've always been terrified of ledges, perilous slippery things, things with fangs and claws that hook onto you—oh, that pull, that silky siren call.

This ledge is no different.

The claws are real, today. They are sharp, they hit true. They hook into the meat of your jaw and they tug and you know the time has come at last to follow. Time to face the truth.

The wall comes down like a sigh, like the inevitability of pain and death and rebirth. And there they are: all the neglected fragments of you. The bits of life you left behind, the shards of your self, of all your past selves. The things you carried, the things you buried. The things you are.

Always the stable one, weren't you? Always the one holding it together, oh so strong, oh so happy. And sure, why not? But there it is, now, that old puffer coat. That short red dress. Those used-up street-worn Converse.

And there, nestled among them: a black lacquered box with five matches.

———

Watch this, watch me now. Watch it all burn.

ONE FOR THE DEMONS

Tell the night I'm coming
With a bag upon my head
Tell the night I'm running
At the things I should have said
Demons, you can chase me
You can find me in your throat
Hold my guts and face me
Hold me hard, I am the rope
Vivisection cannot kill me
I am the master of the blight
Loose the cannibal to fill me
I am coming, tell the night

ACKNOWLEDGMENTS

So many people came with me on this journey and were there with input, information, and encouragement that helped to shape the stories in this book: Joshua McCune, Anna Crowley, Lori Kilkelly, Lily Neve, Zack Paquette, Tracey Keevan, Kip Wilson, Julie Phillipps, Nancy Werlin, Debbie Kovacs, Erin Dionne, Allison Hoch, Karen Day, Kate Messner, William Henry Lewis, Bill Roorbach, John Cusick. My indefatigable agents, Jim McCarthy and Erin Murphy. My brilliant editors, Dan Ehrenhaft and Melissa Ann Singer, and the rest of the magnificent Team Blackstone. My daughters, Kim and Lauren. Without all of you in my life, there would be no life worth having. I truly am the luckiest author and human alive.

To all the skeletons in my past: I salute you. Thank you for the chance to turn my realities into fiction. Without you, I would be a boring human indeed. My appreciation also to the various places where these stories took shape: the Roasted Granola, Bellmont Caffe (look, Rachid, I'm finally done!), Diesel Cafe, Walden Pond (solo swim the long way across: 10/10 dnr), that cool Airbnb studio in downtown Concord called the Grist Mill, and (gone but not forgotten) my Ideal Chair where this whole harebrained scheme began, with my phone to my ear and my best friend on the line. Who'd have thought it would come to this?

Lastly, to all those of you who have cheered me on, expressed your excitement and enthusiasm and eagerness to read the finished book: Here it is. Welcome to the inside of my head. It's dark and kind of fucked up in here, but it's what I've got. Make yourself at home, maybe stick around awhile? I'll be seeing ya.